Deviant Shadows
Tales of the ParAbnormal

By WPaD
(Writers, Poets and Deviants)

Deviant Shadows
Tales of the ParAbnormal

By WPaD
(Writers, Poets and Deviants)

ISBN: ISBN: 9798464110267

Copyright © 2021 WPaD and all authors named in this book
All Rights Reserved

Original cover art by J. Harrison Kemp
of Tenkara Studios, Toronto, Ontario

All stories and poetry in this book remain the property of their respective authors. No individual or agency other than those named may reproduce, copy or publish any part of this book in full or in part, in any medium printed or digital, without the expressed permission of the owner(s) of those works.

par·a·nor·mal /perˈəˈnɔːr.məl/
adjective
Impossible to explain by known natural forces or by science.

ab·nor·mal /abˈnôrməl/
adjective
Not typical, usual, or regular; not normal; deviant.

par·Ab·nor·mal /perˈəbˈnɔːr.məl/
adjective
Atypical paranormal fiction produced by Writers, Poets and Deviants.

Table of Contents

Not Another Ghost Story ~ Poetry by Amy Karian
The Face Under the Ice by Mike Cooley
Lucky Me by Juliette Kings
Anyone for Chess? by Michael Haberfelner
The Bloody Knife by Harpalyce Wilde
The Gazebo by Diana Garcia
The Price of Love by Marla Todd
Charlie by Dave Henderson
A True Story by L.A. Guettler
Essence ~ Poetry by Soleil Daniels
Desert Winds by Juliette Kings
The Girl in the Mirror by Mandy White
Lunatic by R James Turley
Star Crossed by Juliette Kings
Religion Revisited ~ Poetry by Diana Garcia
The Curious Fate of Aaron Dickerson by Brian Callahan
Goin' Medieval by Debra Lamb
8 Seconds by Mike Cooley
Evenings at 1123 Evergreen Street by L.A. Guettler
Let's Get Haunted by Allison Ketchell
Nightmare in the Nursery by R James Turley
A Letter of Disappointment by Amy Karian
Weathered Spirits by David Haunter
Better Than Beethoven by Michael Haberfelner
Blood Witch by Mike Cooley
For Love of the Trees by Harpalyce Wilde
Out, Damn Spot! by Mandy White
Crawl Space by Juliette Kings
New Emotions by R. James Turley

Books by WPaD
Meet the Authors

Not Another Ghost Story
By Amy Karian

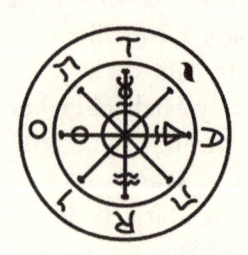

I'm not going to write another ghost story.
No matter what they say.
Not going to write about chains rattling
On a dark and stormy night.
I'm not going to write about
Ghosts who weep and wail
And bang on the walls
While everyone else tries to sleep.
I might write about vampires seeking blood
Or about werewolves seeking friends.
I might write about a Bigfoot and a Chupacabra
Looking for a long lost fishing pole.
But I'm not going to write about ghosts.
Nor about any women in white.
Nor about any spiteful spirits out to write wrongs.
Because I don't want to write another ghost story.
No, thank you.
Not tonight.

The Face Under the Ice
By Mike Cooley

I was walking across the lake, on the way home from Buster's, like I did every Friday night in the winter.

I was dressed warm, and the liquor made me feel warmer. It wasn't cold for winter in Minnesota, but it was cloudless and what little heat there had been during the day was being sucked off the ground. My cabin was about a mile north from my watering hole, which was on the south end of Sackinaw Lake. The shortest path was right across the lake in the winter, and the lake was frozen a foot thick. The air smelled of wood fires and, in the distance, I could hear the thump of the band playing behind me. Ahead of me I could see the glow of the blue light I had left on, so I could find my way back easily. I wasn't a heavy drinker, but when I was hanging with the boys, I did manage to get a little over my limit, from time to time. And this was one of those times.

I must have wandered off my normal path, since I happened upon a patch of crystal-clear ice. Most of the lake was opaque and frosted. I usually just followed my footsteps, since I was the only one nuts enough to walk back and forth over the lake at night. But there were no prints in the snow near me. The clear spot was circular and twenty yards across. I looked down into the lake as I walked. That's when I saw it.

The face.

At first, I thought it was a piece of plastic, frozen into the surface. But then I saw the eyes.

The mouth was moving, as if screaming. And I could see fists battering the ice beside the face, looking up at me.

He wanted out.

My mind wrestled with the thought. *How the hell could someone be alive, under the ice, in the middle of the lake?* I blinked and rubbed my eyes with the palms of my hands, trying to shake the fog of booze loose.

My thoughts tried to make it make sense. *He fell in. There must be a hole nearby. And it must have just happened. He's lucky I showed up.*

I knelt down near the face, which was sparking a hint of memory in my drunken brain. *Where had I seen him before? The store? Duluth? Back at Buster's?*

"Hold on! I'll get something to get you out of there!" I yelled at the pale face beneath the ice and gestured a chopping motion.

The face nodded.

I stood up and turned toward the western shoreline, which was the closest. Then I began to run. My legs pumped hard, and my adrenaline kicked in. *How long could a man last under the ice? Four minutes? There was no chance.* But I ran, nonetheless. To my right, the northern lights danced high in the sky like neon apparitions. Dark-winged birds circled overhead, looking down at me with beady eyes. They were silent, gliding, hoping I would have a heart attack and drop.

When I reached shore, I searched the yards of the cabins for anything I could use. The cabins were shut down for the winter, so the only light I had was from the gibbous moon, which was low in the sky toward the southwest. Most of the yards were covered with snow and the sheds were locked. I was searching the shoreline of the fourth cabin when I found a pickaxe, propped against a wooden wheel as decoration. It was weathered and rusty, but it looked like it might do the job.

I shouldered the pick, then turned and ran back to the clearing in the ice, my lungs bursting from the effort. I dropped the pick and placed my hands on my knees, gasping for air. Sweat ran down from under my knit hat, stinging my grey eyes. The circling birds above me in the sky had drawn closer and were cawing gently like they were urging me on.

I didn't expect to see what I saw.

The face was still there. Eyes wide. Mouth screaming. Fists beating on the underside of the frozen surface.

I showed him the axe. And then started bashing the ice with it, aiming to carve a hole around him and pull him out. My heart was beating like a machine gun, and my brain was still trying to figure out where I had seen him before. Memories flipped by, like cards in a deck, but nothing lined up.

His hands were splayed open, fingers pressing against the frozen sheet. His lips were together and he wasn't blinking. The eyes were haunting. Puzzled. It was almost like he was trying to recognize me, too.

I slammed the pick axe into the ice until my shoulders felt like they were going to give way, walking around in an arc and chopping down until I hit water.

Finally, as I was about to pass out, I had cracked a ring of ice around him. I put the pick down and jumped on the edge of the carved circle. The ice chunk sank down from my weight and slipped underneath the main sheet, leaving an opening.

"Thank the gods!" The man with the face said, sputtering to the surface. He gasped for air, gulping it down eagerly.

I ran over, grabbed his hands, and pulled him out of the lake.

He collapsed onto the ice, then flipped over and lay on his back. "You saved my life."

"How could you possibly live that long? I had to run all the way to shore and then back here, and then dig." I leaned down and looked at his skin. It was pale but not ashen nor blue. His clothes were as familiar as his face.

He stood up. There was a slight glow around him. A sort of bluish aura.

I looked him over. My heartbeat was still loud in my ears. Adrenaline coursed through my veins. The warmth from the whiskey in my belly was wearing off.

"Don't step back. This is where you always step back." The man with the face held up his open palm.

My right foot slid behind me. "I'm not."

I tried to gather my balance by stepping back with my left foot, and I hit the opening in the lake.

"I told you." The familiar face said. Concern rippled across his brow and he reached toward me. The circling ravens had landed near his feet.

The cold water engulfed me as I fell through the opening. And then I was beneath the surface. The man I had saved was above me, and above the ice. He looked like he was floating in the air. His arms were stretched wide and the ravens were circling above him.

I swam up toward the opening in the ice, toward the glow of the moon, but it was closing quickly. Too quickly. As I reached the

surface it froze solid. I could feel my lungs struggling to hang onto my last breath.
 I pressed against the bottom of the sheet of ice, banging on it with my fists, and finally remembered where I had seen his face before.
 The mirror.

Lucky Me
By Juliette Kings
aka The Vampire Maman

"I took the bus from Los Angeles to Sacramento. At the station I saw an old chum of my brother's from high school. He said he'd give me a ride, but then he got fresh. I wasn't going to, you know, I have cash to pay for gas. I'm not... so he dumped me here. I figured if I walked..."

"Get in. You'll be safe. I promise," he said. It had just started to rain. "I have a house by the lake. You can stay the night. Where are you going?"

"Reno," she told him. "I have a teaching job waiting for me. It starts in two weeks."

He found out she'd left a short abusive marriage. Out of the fire into the frying pan. She was too trusting of people, all bright eyed and perky, even after being left on the side of the road by a creepy pervert.

"I'm Val," he said, holding out his hand.

"Eve," she said. "Your hand is colder than mine. You're freezing."

He smiled. She felt safe for the first time in a long time.

"Val. I like that. Is it short for Valentino?"

"Valentine."

"I like that better," said Eve.

They drove for another half hour to a large cabin by the edge of a lake. Cabin was an understatement; this was a 3,000 square foot luxury home.

"Go change," Val told her. "I have something to show you."

She went into one of the bedrooms, feeling as if she'd been there before.

When Eve returned, in drawstring pajama pants and a comfy sweatshirt, she found Val sitting on the couch in the main living area with his laptop on the coffee table in front of him. A glass of red wine was in his hand.

"I feel better. Thanks for picking me up again," said Eve, as she sat down next to Val.

"It's what I do, Eve. Did anyone else pick you up this week?"

"A couple from San Francisco picked me up on Thursday. I had them drop me off in Truckee. Oh, and last Saturday a trucker picked me up. He was hauling a load of furniture to Salt Lake City. I went all the way to Reno with him. Nice guy. He told me about his wedding plans. What did you want to tell me?"

Val turned to the laptop. "Your body was found last week by some Cal Trans workers getting the road ready for winter. They found your suitcase. There were also two other young women, both killed and dumped within a couple weeks of you. Both disappeared from the Sacramento Greyhound station in October of 1987."

"What about Tom?"

"Tom Turner was arrested last night. He wallet was found under the body of one of the other women. He'd also kept souvenirs. Your purse and heart shaped locket were found in his house."

"Wow. I didn't know about the others. Oh, Val. Thank God it is over. What happened to the other two women?"

"They didn't stay," Val said, turning back to the computer. "After the bodies were found, reports came in of a hitchhiker in a red leather jacket, with long blonde hair. She'd been seen on the highway for the past thirty years."

"You know, I don't remember when I go out at night. Not until they drop me off."

"I know, Eve. It's ok."

"I'm glad they arrested the sick bastard."

"So am I. If you'd told me his name earlier, I would have taken care of him myself."

"I didn't remember it until now. Val, do you think I'll go out again?"

"I don't know."

"Do you think I'll move on? I guess, see the light?"

"I can't answer that, but you know you can stay here as long as you want."

"I saw some other ghosts out tonight. They're so lost."

"Donner Party folks?"

"How'd you know?"

"They're always out there."

"What if you go away? Will I have to wander around with them?"

"I won't go away. I'll always be here for you, Eve."

"Lucky me, being picked up by a Vampire."

Val smiled. "Lucky you."

Anyone for Chess?
By Michael Haberfelner

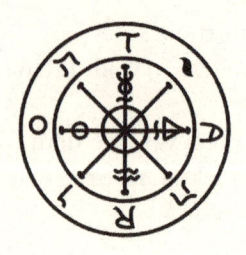

Ah, finally he has noticed the big chess board in the corner of the room – though noticed is hardly the right word, even in its corner it's still prominent enough to attract immediate attention. But alas, chess has so fallen out of favor in the last few decades. My, I wager many of the young ones nowadays don't even know how to play the "King's Game". Yes, with the decline of respect for their rulers, interest for the game has eroded in society. But this man, he's a glimmer of hope. Gradually, he inches toward the long set-up board. There, he touches a piece, then another one, then he caresses a rook, then picks up the queen to inspect her. She's to his liking. He puts her back, and then… he moves a pawn forward two squares. Ok my friend, challenge taken.

This proves to be interesting. His game seems to be all over the place, but he might just be obfuscating his strategy. I'm onto you, my friend, not that I'd ever tell you; I'll just parry your childish attacks for a while and then strike like a viper.

Have I already said this proves to be interesting? Oh I couldn't have been more wrong. Unfortunately, my opponent plays like a bloody amateur. It's mate in three, really… but no, I'll give him the chance for a comeback. After all, I wouldn't want to discourage him with the first game. So this move would give you a good chance to capture my queen in two. Unless you smelled she's just bait of course…

Check mate! I've tried to postpone it as long as I could, but you just fell for all of my ruses. Oh, you want another game. Very well, dear Sir.

Check mate! Oh of course I'm up for one more. Delighted, actually.

Between you and me, I think my new friend is cheating… and that's not even phrased quite right, I *know* he's cheating. I mean it hasn't eluded me that he every so often picks up a piece as if in thought, then puts it back onto a different square. Oh, not always a different square, that would be too obvious, but too often to believe it's just coincidence. And yes, I know it's true to a fact and not just a figment of my imagination, since only yesterday he had both of his bishops on black – now how could that happen in a fair game? Frankly, for his impertinence I should get up and slap him across the face, but alas I cannot, so I guess I just have to accept it for what it is. What I do not understand, though, is what he actually gets out of his cheating. It's not that his cheatings are at all advantageous to his game, they usually lead to nowhere and I still beat him easily. If he follows some bigger scheme, I'd sure like to know about it.

Check mate! Hey my friend, what are you doing, why are you putting the pieces away? Have I discouraged you that much? Come on, I'll give you an advantage the next time. How about I play without a queen? Or without rooks, you know how important they are to my strategy. Well what's this, why do you push all pieces aside? And how could you put such a mundane board game right above the chess board? I mean, Ludo of all things, are you kidding me? The peasant's game?

* * *

"Honey, you've got to see this!"
"See what?"
"Well there, in the painting?"
"What's up with the stupid painting?"
"Well, can't you see?"
"All I can see is that I still don't like it, it brings down the mood of the study."
"How can you say that? It perfectly mirrors the room."
"That's the other thing that brings down the mood of the study – the whole décor, it's so… antique. No wonder people were so depressed in the 19th century."
"But look, there in the back!"
"The chess board, you mean?"
"Yeah. Do you see what happened there?"
"No."

"How it changed from yesterday?"

"Frankly, I avoided looking at the stupid painting yesterday – or all week for that matter. Don't think I've even been to this bloody study more than maybe five times since we moved in."

"Could we get back to the matter at hand? You really can't see what happened in the picture?"

"For fuck's sake, no, and frankly, unless it caught fire, I don't bloody care."

"Let me explain anyhow. Yesterday the pieces on the chess board in the painting were in their initial positions, just like the one on the chess board in the back of the room. Then yesterday out of pure boredom, I moved a pawn on the board – and look what happened in the picture."

"Well, how do you know the pieces were even in their initial positions in the painting?"

"Are you kidding me? The painting didn't just mirror my move, it actually parried my move. That can't be coincidence."

"This is stupid!"

"Look! Look what happened now!"

"What? Have your chess pieces moved some more?"

"Bingo!"

"This is stupid!"

"But just look! You will agree that the painting has changed from yesterday."

"Well… maybe. I didn't pay that much attention."

"Why, can't you see? Yesterday it was just two pawns that have been moved forward. And now, look at the bishop and the knight!"

"Hmmm, ok, they seem to have moved."

"I know! Isn't that amazing?"

"Meh."

"What do you mean, meh? This might be a door to another dimension or something, and you just say… 'meh'?"

"Well, I read this article in Reader's Digest magazine only recently about how in the 19th century they tried to invent mechanical chess machines. You know, like chess computers without, erm, computers. Some of them were pretty elaborate in design. I just figure this is one of them. Nice touch with the painting and everything, I give you that."

"But how would that work? A chess computer without a computer?"

"That was the problem, it didn't. These mechanical chess machines would be good for making a few basic moves over and over, but nothing beyond that. There was an instance though, where this inventor had a dwarf inside his machine who actually made all the moves…"

"You're not taking this seriously!"

"Well… no. Still, just telling you what I've read."

"You know what? I'll prove you wrong. I'm going to finish this game."

"You want to play chess? Against a painting?"

"If that's what it takes to convince you."

"But you're crap at chess."

"Honey, you'll have to come see this!"

"Well somebody's sounding triumphant today."

"Indeed I am. Look at the painting."

"Erm, what am I supposed to see?"

"Why isn't it obvious? The painting, it won!"

"It won?"

"Indeed it did. And I guess it's time now for you to take back what you said the other day."

"Oh I totally take that back… you're not just crap at chess, you're pathetic!"

"You're still playing against that painting?"

"First it was mere curiosity, now it's my pride."

"Oh for fuck's sake, you do know you're being pranked, right? Like with a dwarf in that chess machine I've been telling you about."

"So where would that dwarf hide?"

"Honey, we're in the 21st century, technology has evolved a bit since then. Also, I think you're not supposed to say dwarf anymore."

"Honey, won't you come to bed?"

"Not yet, I… still have some reading to do."

"Another one of those chess books?"

"What else?"

"What else indeed. You've become really obsessed with the whole affair."

"And wouldn't you? How the hell can it be that I lose every fucking game?"

"I didn't know you were such a sore loser."

"I'm not, it's just… well, people have called me intelligent. I should be able to not fall for all of my opponent's tricks at least."

"You know, just maybe… chess isn't your game. Maybe your strength isn't strategy but… cunning. Maybe you should try a game of Ludo."

"So how did your game of Ludo go?"

"It didn't go at all. My opponent in the picture just pushed over all the tokens."

"Erm… you know when I suggested Ludo it was thought as a joke?"

"What does it matter? What I know now is that there's some intelligence on the other side of this painting that goes beyond just playing games. And maybe his playing chess with me was just an attempt to get in touch with me. If only I could communicate with whoever it is on the other side."

"Yeah, if only there was a board game that used letters for its tokens…"

* * *

Well, finally. I almost thought we'd be playing board games forever. You know you're really thick, my friend. You really think I enjoy playing chess that much? And with an opponent as inferior as you, too? And doing only a couple of moves a day when I could have defeated you in minutes? But this… Scrabble, is what it's called? This Scrabble has opportunities. Frankly, I would have thought humankind has evolved a little more by now when it comes to means of communication – but heck, I'm just inhabiting a painting hanging on a wall, I'll take whatever I can.

Ah, you're catching on, I have to give you that. I really almost lost hope during our games of chess, but here you are, preparing for the ritual as if it was for your benefit. My, God bless gullibility!

* * *

"Do we have any candles?"

"Why do you need candles? Don't say you want to surprise me with a romantic dinner!"

"No, silly, you…"

"…and you blew it! Well, wouldn't have been a surprise anyway after you've asked me."

"Well, do we have candles or don't we?"

"What do you need them for?"

"Well, the painting. It told me…"

"Wait! You're talking to the thing now? This is stupid!"

"Not, erm, 'talking' talking, more like… well, the Scrabble was your idea."

"Oh Jesus, I was just testing how far you'd take it – and obviously you outdid yourself this time."

"Well, don't you want to find out what's on the other side?"

"Other side? What the fuck are you talking about? Someone's playing an elaborate prank on you. And you fell for it, hook, line and sinker."

"Well, do we have candles?"

"Kitchen, second cupboard from the right, top drawer."

"Thanks!"

"…and next thing you'll also ask me for a piece of chalk."

"How… how did you know?"

"Oh boy. And let me guess, you'll have to draw a chalk circle, sit inside naked while reciting some magic spells."

"No, silly… I won't be naked. That would be stupid."

"And this whole plethora of clichés – doesn't this at all suggest to you that you're being had?"

"So, do we have chalk?"

"So, are you coming?"

"Where to?"

"Well, to the study. For the ritual."

"You're actually going through with this?"

"Why of course. Why would I stop now? Want to come?"

"Well, it sure is tempting, just to see your stupid face when you realize you've been pranked. But then again, I love you and I don't want to see you humiliated… so I'll take a rain check. Thanks anyway."

* * *

What's… what's this? Why do I feel all different? Actually, I don't feel at all anymore, nothing at all. I also… I don't breathe. Am I dead? But dead men, they can't see, and I can. On the other hand, I can't blink. Weird, and yet my eyes don't fill with water. Come to think of it, I don't feel I even have eyes – and yet I can see, I just have no control over where to look, just straight ahead, as if I was a camera kept perfectly still. Also, I don't feel any of my limbs, as if I just didn't have them. But I can see my study lying plain before me, just from an odd angle. You know, if I didn't know better I'd say I'm looking into the room exactly from where that painting of ours is hanging…

* * *

"Who are you?"
"That's kind of hard to…"
"And what are you doing in our study?"
"You won't believe…"
"And where's my husband? Why are you wearing his clothes?"
"Listen, it's the painting…"
"Wait, you're the one who pranked my husband with that painting? Get out of my house!"
"No wait, you don't understand…"
"You know what, stay! I'll call the police."
"But I can explain…"
"Let go of me you…"
"Ouch! What was that for?"

* * *

Good God, why is my wife getting into a struggle with that stranger? If only I could hear them! Hey, don't push my wife! If only I could help! But it seems I'm nailed to the wall. Hey, don't run!

Oh my God, the Scrabble pieces on the chess board have just spelled out my thoughts! How is that possible? Can it be…

* * *

"Who are you?"
"I think I can help you find your husband."
"Oh for fuck's sake, not another one!"
"Another one? I'm not sure I follow you."
"Of course you do. You think you're the first who promises to 'bring him back alive' – for a price of course. I don't even know how many faces of gumshoes and bounty hunters I've smashed this door into by now."
"I assure you, I don't ask for money…"
"That'd be a new one. But listen, I trust in the work of the police…"
"But they don't know what I know."
"Riiight…"

"Like, the last time you saw your husband was when he went into your study, right? And in the study hangs a painting that's pretty much a mirror image of the study."

"You... how do..."

"May I come in then?"

"You... you've redecorated?"

"The whole room, it always depressed me with all that antique furniture."

"But the painting, where's the painting?"

"I burnt it."

"You WHAT?"

"Oh, it was too depressing – a reminder of my missing husband. That said, it's not that it was worth anything much, it was actually just a prankster's toy. You know it could spell words with the Scrabble pieces on the chess board?"

"Words? Like what?"

"All sorts of words, but in the end it was just 'help' and 'help me'."

"And you ignored it?"

"Ignored it? It drove me up the walls, what me being worried sick about the disappearance of my husband anyway and..."

"You know those were probably messages from your husband..."

"Are you kidding? Are you FUCKING kidding me?"

"You see, your husband's soul was trapped in the painting because of a ritual he performed..."

"How could I have been so blind! You're one of the pranksters, aren't you? The ones that drove my husband out of his mind by sending him messages over the painting..."

"I assure you, it's no prank."

"Get out of my house – NOW!"

"I'll go, I'll go – just please take my card, and promise you'll call me if you change your mind!"

"I've just got three words for you: This is stupid!"

THE BLOODY KNIFE
By Harpalyce Wilde

It had happened again — the bloody knife lay beside me on my pillow. I gagged and ran to the bathroom, barely lifting the toilet lid before my stomach tried to exit through my mouth.

When I got done cleaning myself up, I noticed a text on my phone from my mom. "Caidence, we have to talk about your rent money. I can't get it to you until the 15th." My mom, the school teacher, was the only one I knew who used proper caps, punctuation, and spelling in all her texts. It made communication with her seem slightly weird and overly formal.

I sighed. I love my mom, but it's complicated. My mind began to cycle on how to pay the rent, who I could ask for a loan to tide me over until mom could come up with it. In a way it was a welcome distraction from the more disturbing mystery that waited for me in the other room. Sighing again, I went to clean up the mess.

The knife in question was a long, broad-bladed butcher-knife, razor sharp and covered in dark-clotted blood, with an ornate, old fashioned silver handle. Gingerly, I picked up the entire pillow, folded it around the knife and stuffed it into a trash bag. I added a couple cans of expired green beans to weigh it down when I threw it into the water. I'd need to pick a different dump location this time. Just in case.

My eyes scanned the tiny apartment carefully for any other signs of blood, or anything else out of place. A footprint, or a fingerprint — any clue about who'd left the bloody knife and what message it was supposed to convey.

But like all the other times, there wasn't a single detail out of place. My front door was still locked and the chain was on. The grimy windows were wedged shut with dowel rods. There was no sign of how an intruder could have entered to leave their gristly gift. Like a locked room mystery, I couldn't see any solution.

My mom thought it was some ex of mine, or some creepy stalker who'd found me on the internet. But I don't have an ex — at least not that I know of — I'd hardly even dated. I know that's hard to believe, but I'd never been that serious with anyone. No matter how hard I tried, I couldn't think of a single person who'd dedicate their life to freaking me out. Especially nobody with the ninja-skills to pull this off. But now that I'd been discovered here, it was time to change my name again and move on.

I thought of my futile dreams — of finding a steady job and friends I could keep for more than a few months. A normal life, like it had been with me and mom, before that first time... For a moment I was tempted to say 'screw it all', and just stay here to see what happened. But then my eyes fell upon the wrapped bundle with its threatening, bloody contents; and I sighed with resignation.

No. It was safer to run, and keep running.

***

After I'd disposed of the bundle, I went back to the apartment to pack. I'd been moving around so often that I didn't have much stuff. Two suitcases held my clothes, and four cardboard boxes bulged with the rest. I jammed everything into the tiny hatchback of my beater car, and strapped my guitar case into the passenger seat.

Checking the time, I decided to hit my favorite busking stop for the early rush. Maybe I could pick up enough cash to afford a cheap motel tonight. It wasn't ideal, but nothing about my life could be called ideal.

I found a spot that was convenient and out of the way, and spread an old blanket on the concrete. I set out the battered black top hat I'd picked up for a dime from a yard sale, and propped a few of my CDs nearby. They weren't great quality since I'd recorded in the train station bathroom with my phone instead of a studio. But the artwork looked nearly professional and a few people bought them — more out of pity than love of my musical talent, I suspected. Still, it gave people an excuse to drop a ten in my hat instead of just a handful of nickels and quarters. What they did with the CD after they paid for it, I didn't care.

Then I gave myself over to the music, running through a lot of my basic material, covers from the fifties, sixties, and seventies. My only legacy from the bastard who'd gotten my mom pregnant then moved on — an entire box of old vinyl records that I played halfway to death in my teen years. I put my own spin on the music, of course.

As the crowds scurried past, I threw in the single song I'd written myself, a minor-key lament in the general musical style of Queen. It was fitting today, as it related the feelings of a seventeen year old girl who'd been framed for murder and had to go on the run. I'd written it in the week after the bloody knife first appeared on my pillow. It ended badly for the girl, of course. In my defense, that had been a really morbid phase of my life.

Not that it's improved much in the following three years...

But somehow, occupying my fingers allowed my mind to roam free and work on the problems that beset me. Music had become my best friend and solace, and now I worked all my loneliness and sadness into my chords and added just a hint of husky vocal to the mix. I made the guitar sob and ache; and when I thought to look up now and then, I'd notice a teardrop or sniffle from a lingering commuter. Generally followed by a buck or two in the hat, and twice, a CD sale.

The makeup of the crowds gradually changed as the orange sun sank toward the horizon. The last of the commuters scurried past, drab and exhausted, to make way for a different crowd. Replacing them, strolling groups of laughing couples dressed in bright colors, bound into the city for a meal at a restaurant, or a night out dancing.

A beat cop patrolled past, giving me a dark and promising scowl before he turned to smile and give directions to an expensively clad tourist. I got the hint and started packing up before he could circle the block. Even camping in my car under a bridge would be better than spending the night — and possibly longer — in jail. With quick, efficient fingers, I gathered the pile of CDs into my briefcase and strapped the guitar back into its seat before starting the engine.

* * *

I frowned when I counted my hat money — I'd hit only the end of rush hour, and there were other buskers to compete against. Which meant there was plenty for a burger and shake from the local drive thru, but not quite enough for a motel.

But it was summer and we were having a stretch of mild, dry weather. I decided I'd take the tent to a campground and unroll my sleeping bag there. Then, I'd figure tomorrow out when it arrived. So I ran through the drive-thru, and rolled into the campground just as the long summer twilight was fading from pink-orange to scarlet.

"This was a good idea," I told myself as I rolled down my window to pay the kid for a bundle of firewood. A night under the stars. Wood smoke, wind through the trees, sounds of nature. I had plenty of quarters to run the hot water and clean up in the morning.

But when I pulled my box of camping gear out of the hatchback, my hammer had gone missing. The ground was hard; and without it, I couldn't get the tent stakes in. So I sat in the middle of my tent and just started to cry for a few minutes. Then, since that didn't get me any closer to a roof over my head before night fell, I wiped my face dry, put on my best smile, and headed toward the tent next door. Surely someone would have a hammer I could borrow. I could see a faint glow inside, so I knew that someone was home.

Once I got over there, I stood awkwardly, trying to figure out to knock on a canvas wall. After a bit, I just tried clearing my throat loudly a few times.

The tent flap twitched and opened.

His eyes were the first feature that hit me — deep hazel pools flecked with amber. Solid cheekbone structure, honey-browned skin, just a manly hint of stubble without being unkempt. Adorable cleft chin. Middling brown hair, a bit too short for my taste. And a quizzical smile on too-sculpted lips. Nice pecs, too... Pretty, but not quite simmering hot, more like somebody's dad. But nice.

I shook myself and laughed a bit nervously. "Umm, hi. I'm Cai — I'm from the tent next door... I mean... that pile of poles that's supposed to be a tent, except I forgot to bring anything to pound my tent stakes..."

The man's eyes were glued to me and his smile had grown a bit warmer, but he didn't speak, just looked me over, slow-like. In a way that was starting to make me feel a little weird.

I rushed ahead, wondering if I should have tried the RV with the screaming baby instead. "So anyway, I was wondering if I could borrow a hammer or a hatchet or something..."

"Oh. Sure." Mister nice pecs held out a hand. "I'm Jay, by the way."

I giggled, I couldn't help it. Get a grip, Caidence, I told myself sternly, or he'll think you're flirting. "Oh, I'm sorry. It's just... Jay and Cai... ye-ahhh..." I trailed off, having totally failed to save face. "Because they... rhyme... Nevermind." By now I'm sure I was blushing, but Jay acted like he didn't notice.

"Honey, do you have your hammer?" Jay called into the tent.

"It's right he-ere, tiger." The masculine voice replied from within. A head popped out — deep brown skin and almond-dark eyes, with a pair of silver bar piercings over his left eyebrow. "Oh, who's this?"

"I'm your neighbor." I put on my best smile.

His look, up and down me, conveyed the message clearly – Jay was not up for grabs to some rando girl who showed up and fluttered at him.

"I, uh… forgot mine." I smiled apologetically and dropped my eyes a moment – message received.

He ducked back into the tent and then handed me the tool, flashing densely tattooed sleeves that covered both forearms with bright, tropical birds. Feeling more awkward than ever, I made a few more polite noises and fled to finish setting up my campsite.

* * *

I didn't wake to find the knife next to me, though I'd been dreading the possibility before I even opened my eyes. The dapples of light dancing on my tent's wall and the raucous croaking of ravens reminded me that I wasn't in my apartment.

Usually after the knife appeared, I had some grace period before it happened again. Sometimes it was a few months, until I'd nearly put the gruesome thing out of my mind and begun to believe my nightmare was over. But other times it appeared every week like clockwork, especially if I'd failed to heed the warning and move along to a new place. As far as I could tell, there was no pattern to it. It was a macabre riddle with no solution.

After hitting the campground's facilities, I wandered over to watch the nearby creek rumble past for a while, then looped back toward my tent. I hadn't decided if I'd stay another night, putting off the inevitable hunt for a new place to settle. Eventually, I wandered back to my campsite, where Jay and his boyfriend Andrew offered me coffee, pancakes, and bacon. They looked so normal and innocent that I nearly took them up on it.

But they looked so happy together that I didn't want to bring them down with my problems, which they'd inevitably try (unsuccessfully) to help me solve. They totally looked like the type to enjoy riding to the rescue of a poor little lost girl. Been there, done that, don't need any more T-shirts.

So I dismantled the tent and bundled my camping stuff into the hatchback. I gave Jay a final, apologetic smile before driving off in search of a café. He smiled back and waved goodbye, then went back to pouring real maple syrup on his breakfast.

The local café's food was probably a lot less tasty than what I would have gotten at the campground, I mused sadly. I lingered over it, letting the grandmotherly server refill my coffee cup over and over again. The bill would eat up the rest of my cash reserves, so I'd have to hustle if I wanted any lunch.

The breakfast crowd swelled, then dwindled, and the table busser was starting to give me searching looks — it was time to move on. I stood and emptied my pockets of crumpled bills and coins, just as the local sheriff rolled into the parking lot. I passed him uneasily on the way to my car, keeping my eyes on the ground, afraid that my guilty secrets would be readable upon my face.

"Right or left?" I asked myself as I pulled to the two-lane highway that ran past the roadside diner. Right led back toward the city. Left led further out into the wilderness, eventually turning toward the coastal beaches. I pondered which way made more sense to go — earning some fast cash would be easier in the city; yet the urge to just drive into the wilderness and get lost was almost overwhelming.

Finally a honk behind me, from a Volvo with two brightly colored kayaks strapped to the roof, woke me from my stupor. Flipping on my turn signal, I headed right. I'd earn some gas money, first. Then I could wander around and look for my next home.

* * *

But I'd only gone five miles before I saw a woman with a yellow day-pack walking alongside the road. A pickup had slowed down to pace her, with two middle-aged men leering at her from within. The woman flashed a worried glance over her shoulder at them and walked faster.

I didn't even think — just slowed down to flip a U-ey and sped back toward her. I pulled in front of the pickup truck, jammed on the brakes, and honked. Then I opened the door and yelled the first thing that came into my head. "There you are, Susie! Get in — we're late!"

The woman froze for just one moment and her eyes flickered between the brewing trouble with the men, and the crazy strange girl who acted like she knew her.

Not waiting for her to decide, I grabbed my guitar case from its place of honor in the front seat, and slid it into the back. A second later, the woman jumped into my car. She was young — about my age,

I guessed. Pretty, with smooth olive skin and raven-black hair, with long legs scrunched in my tiny front seat.

"Gun it." She settled her pack at her feet and fumbled with the seatbelt while I shoved the hatchback into gear. The men in the pickup were staring after us, but didn't look like they were going to give chase.

"Um, I hope you have some gas money." We were headed away from the city, now; but I remembered there was a mini-mart gas station across from the café where I'd had breakfast. "So, where are you headed?"

"How did you know my name?" The woman's voice was hard and suspicious. I turned to look at her, and she was pointing a knife at my face.

In one hyper-focused moment I saw the wide butcher blade, the intricate silverwork of the handle, and I recognized it. Except for being clean, it was identical to the one I kept finding on my pillow. I screamed and swerved the car, almost losing control of it and landing us in a ditch.

"Jeez!" The woman pulled the knife away, glaring at me like I'm the stupid one. "Look out, I nearly cut you."

"Where did you get that knife?" Panting, I slowed the hatchback and turned its nose down a random dirt road.

"I asked first. You answer my question, and I'll answer yours." She was still gripping the butcher knife in a vaguely menacing fashion. "How did you know my name?"

I followed the dirt road until we were out of sight of the main highway, then put it in park and turned the engine off before replying. "I didn't. I just made up a random name so those guys would think we knew each other. They looked like trouble."

But, it hadn't been completely random, I realized, even as I said it. I'd called out the name of my imaginary twin sister, who I hadn't thought about in years. According to mom, once upon a time, I'd been lonely for siblings I didn't have. For several years, I'd been convinced that Susie was real. Only after the school sent me to a child psychologist had I stopped talking about her. When I'd realized the other kids wouldn't play with me because they thought my behavior was weird, I'd made myself stop seeing her everywhere. Just shut her out.

But Susie was wearing a strange expression. The knife had dropped, forgotten, into her lap and she was eyeing me very strangely.

"Caidy?" Her voice was weak, and her eyes were round and scared. "I-it can't be. You were never real... I imagined you, d-didn't I?"

"I... I imagined you too, Susie — you were my twin." A chill ran through me. Even though we looked nothing alike, there was something about her that seemed so familiar. "This is too weird..."

"I know, right?" Susie laughed, an uneasy chuckle; but she was still studying me with fascination. I found myself doing the same, studying her.

After an uncomfortable minute of silence, I decided it was time to change the topic. "So, you were going to tell me about the knife. What do you know about it?"

Susie gave me a different look — judging, weighing — for a long, long time. Finally she nodded and pulled out a wad of cash. "Okay, I'll tell you. But this is going to require a whole lotta booze."

* * *

After buying provisions, we drove for a few hours. Then we turned down a narrow track to an unmarked beach. Susie piled the campfire wood we'd bought, along with a few chunks of driftwood, into a roaring fire while I assembled the tent, pounding in the stakes with a rock. We ate our take-out burgers and listened to the hiss of pebbles in the surf. A fog was rolling in, muffling sound and shrinking the world to the radius of our firelight.

"So. What's the story?" We sat on my camp stools in front of my tent, eating food that Susie had paid for. I still couldn't quite get over us being some sort of spirit-twins, a theory that Susie had gone on and on about as we drove. It had given me time to think — I needed to find out what she knew before I gave up my own guilty secret. "What do you know about that knife?"

"I was seventeen. It seemed like a good idea at the time." Susie laughed abruptly and took a long drink from the bottle of cheap bourbon.

"What did?" I was already drunker than I wanted to be, and she'd had three times more. I wasn't sure how she was still sitting upright.

"Stealing the knife." Susie waved a hand somewhat vaguely. The knife in question had vanished back into her backpack. I could see the very top of the handle peeking out through the zipper. She saw me looking doubtful. "Now look. I didn't steal it for the monetary value. I needed it... to get revenge."

She'd said the words flatly, but they sent a chill down my spine that had nothing to do with the damp night air. Abruptly, she upended the liquor bottle over the fire, pouring out the rest. Blue flames leapt and hissed, throwing wild, dancing shadows across the driftwood logs surrounding us.

Susie spoke as if she'd forgotten I was sitting next to her. The details poured out of her, of a trusted family friend who'd been tutoring her. He'd put his hands on her, had his way with her. She'd wanted to tell her parents but he'd convinced her they wouldn't believe her. The attacks had continued, worse every week as he'd grown certain of his power over her.

Until the day he'd tried it after she stole the knife. The antique blade had seemed to possess some sort of mystical power over him. He'd been paralyzed by the very sight of it, as if frozen by a magic spell. Susie had slashed his throat open, and as his life bled out and his eyes glazed with death, she'd just sat staring at the bloody knife in her hand.

"When I heard someone coming I just... I wished it away, as hard as I could." Susie's voice was harsh and low, a bitter monotone. "By the time the police found me, it had vanished. They found me covered in blood and crying. But when they found no murder weapon, they decided he must have been killed by an intruder, who had then fled."

Susie turned big, haunted eyes toward me over the crackling flames. "I probably shouldn't be telling you this, but since that day, I've kind of felt like a superhero. Like, maybe my life had a mission, a calling. Like... I could be this messed up little girl, you know? Or I could choose to do something about the problem, so the same thing didn't happen to more little girls."

I nodded, licked my lips. A distant foghorn sounded, low and ominous. "So the knife — it paralyzes them?"

"It seems to." Susie shrugged. "When I bring it out, they just stand there like statues. And every time I've used it, once it's covered with their blood it just vanishes. It's just like... magic, I guess. Then, the next day it's back again, but clean — as if it had never been used."

"E-every time?" I stared at Susie, not sure if what I felt was horror or admiration. "How many times have you used the knife?"

She gave me a fierce look, as if my tone had upset her; and maybe it had been a bit harsh... "I've tracked down twenty-three monsters — creeps who wouldn't take no for an answer, who stalked me, who tried to drug my drink. They each did their best to hurt me, and I'm not sorry for a single one."

"Was the last time a couple nights ago?" It was my turn to stare levelly at Susie, waiting for her answer.

"Y-yeah, how did you know?" She stared back at me, looking spooked as I felt.

I shivered at the weirdness of the situation as chills ran over my skin. "Because, twenty-three times over the past three years, a bloody knife has shown up on my pillow."

* * *

After that night, Susie and I parted ways. We decided it would be safer for both of us if we didn't exchange phone numbers, or ever contact each other again. It didn't matter — I knew we'd always have a connection.

And now that I'd learned I wasn't being stalked, I decided it was time to settle down. Time to get a real job, and actually get to know a place. Decorate my apartment with more stuff than would fit into my car. Meet some people; maybe date, if I could find a decent guy. I picked a town near a deep body of water, and called my mom to give her my new address. She was thrilled to hear that my "problem" had been solved, and she promised to visit as soon as she could.

The bloody knife was there on my pillow again, this morning. I smiled as I thought of Susie, my special, superhero twin. Carefully, I wrapped the disposable plastic pillowcase around the knife and tucked it into my backpack. On my way to work, I'd drop it into the center of the Columbia river.

As long as I was careful, no one would ever learn our secret.

THE GAZEBO
By Diana Garcia

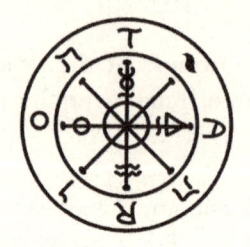

Lottie Prescott stood under the elm tree. The twinkling lights of the gazebo made her forget about her past. Night breezes, like gentle nimble fingers, combed her russet hair creating velvet curls. The breath and waft of jasmine envelope her in shadow.

She remembers the first time she let Apache-Ted run the ivory comb through her wet hair as she bathed. His brown pants wet at the knees where he reverently knelt behind her head, which rested on the soapy edge of the wooden tub. Large calloused brown hands reverently and delicately handled the tresses; as if they would break or cause pain if he accidently pulled or tugged.

He never initiated sexual advances toward Lottie. His veneration of her was palpable. She loved him best. He was quiet and strong. She always made the first move toward him. This gentle beast of a man was gifted to her years ago by an arrogant Captain Randall passing through with his rugged army regiment, on their way to fight and slaughter in some Indian war.

Apache-Ted, of the Tonto tribe, was being dragged by rope at the time. The captain, under assignment from General George Crook had mounted the Bloody Basin Campaign. They claimed to have killed only the renegade Apache, yet many innocent Yavapai were decimated and were purposely not mentioned in the written reports of that bloody encounter. Apache-Ted, their only prisoner, had been hunted and caught on the Yavapai ancestral lands known to the whites as Turret Peak. He sported a deep scar on the left side of his face which deepened when he growled and yipped at terrified onlookers as he was dragged through the Arizona town, popularly touted as "Everybody's Home Town!"

Lottie Prescott stood with the other soiled doves to watch the uninvited procession. She caught the Captain's eye. She stood tall and proud in the scorch of heat and rising dust. Her grim visage melded with the cruel Arizona landscape. He was intrigued by her ivory and russet hatred and dismounted as he ordered his men to rest for an hour. Never pausing to speak or even to look Lottie in the eye, the captain grabbed her by the arm and pulled her inside and upstairs. Women were his weakness and this dove made him want to forget the mass murder he and his men had recently wrought.

Later, he gifted Apache-Ted to her for her sexual services, the likes which the captain had never experienced. He was surprised when she asked for his Indian prisoner in exchange for payment. He paid with a glad heart and with promises to see her again. The Indian was a gift that was never his to give, but he ordered his men to never speak of the exchange. It was an easy thing for his men to forget the exchange since it was only one of the many things they were ordered never to mention, like their destruction of the gentle Yavapai. Forgotten to the winds.

A few years later Apache-Ted died in her arms. He was stabbed multiple times by the unscrupulous vigilante and Indian killer, John B. Townsend. He was the disgraced resentful scout that had recently been sacked by General Crook during the Tonto campaigns. A renowned tracker and hunter of Indians in the central and desert region of Arizona, Townsend was known for his hatred of Apaches and attacked their rancherias in the Tonto every chance he could. Apache-Ted had dared to put himself between Lottie and Townsend's attempted vicious defilement of her. The night before Lottie and Apache-Ted had agreed to flee the town and start a life together. They had planned too late, not able to foresee what was to come.

This was her spot, under the tree, always.

She enjoyed watching young lovers kissing in the gazebo, especially at twilight. Once, when the lights were not on, the moon glow shimmered upon a passionate couple's embrace. For Lottie, the vision was dream-like, beguiling. She stepped out of the shadows. The amorous woman, while her neck was being nuzzled, tilted her head, just so, and saw Lottie looking back at her. The woman whispered something to her lover. They both ran away in terror. Lottie was bereft.

She had been seen. Without turning Lottie reached back with her hand and sought the rough calloused hand of Apache-Ted.

Years before, Lottie tried to explore beyond the park square, but she was locked in place between the gazebo and the tree.

She forgets that remembering her murky past returns her to the gallows, her haunted past, where the gazebo presently stands. It is now the town bandstand. She prefers standing under the tree, the farthest she is able to be from the gallows, with her invisible tether. The gazebo and the tree are the eternal prison for she and Apache-Ted, her shadow, her protector, who stands eternally by her side.

Lottie, feeling Apache-Ted's death rattle as he lay in her arms, looked up at the scowling twisted expression that Townsend directed at her as he stood over the tableau vivant, blood still dripping from his hands and knife. His heavy breathing echoed loudly in her ears. Lottie never realizing that it was she who made the ear-piercing howl, flew at Townsend and grabbed the gun from his holster before he knew what was happening. He never felt the bullet between his eyes. He was a disgraced scout, but here in "Everybody's Home Town!" he was considered the hero Indian killer. Lottie was hauled away to the gallows by her long red hair as people kicked and spat in frenzied rage.

* * *

These days, the gazebo is festooned with twinkling electric lights, and beneath them, the orchestra plays their gay and patriotic music during ice cream socials and town picnics. Modern tourists are oblivious to the Lottie and Apache-Ted of long ago. Lottie, the historical town's notorious soiled dove, swings to-and-fro in the golden glint of the sun's reflection, visible if you look long enough.

They never hear the creaking rope as it rubs on splintered wood, nor do they hear nor behold the angry mob chanting for her to hang and die.

Yet, the history of this old Arizona town replays itself, endlessly; and the orchestra plays on.

*Note from the author: this short story is a work of fiction, great liberties were taken by me; however, there is some history about the Bloody Basin, Captain Randall, and of course, General Crook. Also, John B. Townsend is known as the "Jack-the-Ripper" of Yavapai County, Arizona.

The Price of Love
By Marla Todd

"He stole my heart," she said.

I looked up at the pretty blonde woman in the pink silk blouse. She brushed back a pretty curl that had fallen across her big blue eyes. I had no time for her kind.

"I don't deal in love potions or revenge. If you'd like I know a few other Witches I could recommend. They're quite good."

"You don't understand. He literally stole my heart. I was supposed to have a transplant a few days ago and the bastard stole my new heart."

She opened the top few buttons of her shirt to reveal a long line of stitches. "I was on the operating table, ready to have this pitiful damaged heart of mine removed, when the donor heart vanished. It literally vanished out of thin air, right there in the hospital, in front of the doctors. He said he'd steal my heart, but I never knew the bastard could actually be so ruthless."

Then I noticed the oxygen tank she was wheeling behind her.

She pulled up a barstool and sat down next to me. "I know your rates are extremely high, but so is your success rate. I want my heart back. Will you take the job?"

* * *

Her name was Ava. She looked exhausted, and frankly, extremely ill, so I offered to take her home.

"How'd you know I didn't take my own car here?" she asked.

"I'm a Witch. I know things. Besides, you're in no condition to drive, and you don't seem like a reckless person."

Ava's home was a modest house in a modest middle class neighborhood. Across the street a couple of guys were working on what looked like a '68 Charger. Four middle school aged boys sat on the porch next door eating ice cream bars. Scooters and bicycles lay on the lawn in front of them. Two cats, an orange tabby and a solid black kitty sat on Ava's doorstep. They both stood up when they saw us. I reached down to pet them.

"Meet Mr. Snickers and Mr. Darcy." As the black one wound around my legs and meowed, Ava scratched the orange one behind his ears. "Hey Darcy. How's my sweet baby?"

I helped her inside with oxygen tank. She kicked off her shoes by the front door, and I left mine by the door as well. We were greeted by a tall brown eyed guy, about thirty years old, with brown wavy hair and a short, neat beard.

"Devin, this is Isolde. Isolde this is my fiancé, Devin. Isolde is the one I told you about. She's going to help find my heart."

They led me to a living room filled with mid-century modern style furniture all done in blues and yellows with touches of orange. Original art and 1970's movie posters hung on the wall.

I look at family photos on a bookcase shelf.

"That's my brother Blake," said Ava. "He's in the Coast Guard."

I smiled. "He looks like you."

"Our parents passed away from Covid-19, early in the pandemic. If I die… I'm all he has. We don't have any other family."

"I'll find your heart, Ava," I said. "Blake won't be alone." I wasn't sure if that was going to happen, but I had to stay positive.

I sat in a blue chair. Devin brought out beers for him and me, while Ava had a glass of sparkling water.

I started in on the questions. "Ava, tell me why you think Jon Blanken might have stolen your heart. What was your relationship? What happened to make him want to take your heart? Who are his friends and associates? Are they also into the occult or magic? Do you know where he is now?"

Ava had mentioned his name in the bar and again in the car. She told me Jon Blanken dabbled in the occult, but his name didn't ring a bell with me.

Ava gave an uncomfortable glance at Devin.

"It's ok, honey," said Devin, taking Ava's hand.

Standing in the corner was the faint image of a woman wearing a black dress and rather long colorful scarf. I knew Ava and Devin couldn't see her.

"Go on, Ava," I said, ignoring the apparition, who was now waving her hands at me.

Then Ava took a sip of water and told me about Jon Blanken.

It was the age-old story of a young woman swept off her feet by a charming, handsome man who seemed as rich as he was sexy.

Ava didn't have any clear photos of him. Blanken refused to have his photo taken. He'd laugh it off and make jokes about it. When they were together, he'd take her phone, saying something about his business and that he didn't want to be tracked.

Jon Blanken dazzled and bewitched Ava with his charming ways and his wealth. He controlled her every move. He changed the way she dressed and fixed her hair. It was as if he was grooming her to be his own perfect woman. He demanded perfection in the most loving of ways, or at least his version of perfection. Ava was in an abusive relationship that had come on so slowly and methodically that she didn't even know it.

Then one day she told him she was going to a job interview, for her dream job, and Jon Blanken said no. Then Ava evaluated the situation and left.

Jon Blanken begged her to return, then he began to use threats. Then he vanished.

Ava moved on with her life. A year later she met Devin. It clicked. She became ill. Devin stayed with her. Then Devin asked Ava to marry him.

Jon Blanken contacted her when her name was put on the donor list. He was angry she'd become ill, especially after all he'd done for her. What he said didn't make any sense to Ava. She refused to meet with him. He threatened her, then it was over. She didn't hear from him again, but she was still frightened and more than frightened – she was angry.

I asked her where he was now. Ava didn't know. She and Devin had looked and done the usual Internet searches, but they couldn't find a trace of Jon Blanken. It was as if he'd never existed. Ava and Devin even drove by Blanken's house, or where his house used to be. The large home had burned to the ground; the beautiful gardens that once surrounded it were now dead. None of the neighbors knew what happened or where he'd gone. Property records led nowhere. The Blanken house belonged to a family trust with apparently no living members since 1954. The state was trying to find heirs with no luck, and if no heirs were found, the property would eventually be put up for public auction.

At that point I was going to ask why Ava thought Blanken was into the occult when Mr. Snickers and Mr. Darcy started playing with some beaded fringe on my bag. The two cats knocked it open and out rolled my crystal ball.

"You know my dear," said a voice behind me, "you ought to be more careful with your orb."

Ava and Devin gasped, and both looked shocked as if they'd seen a ghost. I smiled. They had seen a ghost. It was Charlie, the ghost who sometimes resides in my crystal ball.

Charlie, who refuses to go his given name of Charles, looks like the dashing leading man right out of a 1930's romantic comedy. He stood with his million dollar smile, pencil thin mustache, and dark hair brushed back off his face, and bowled us all over with presence. At least that was his goal.

"Oh, right. Ava, Devin, this is Charlie. He helps me out sometimes. Charlie is a ghost," I said.

"Sometimes? Oh please, Isolde, I help you out ALL of the time." Then he turned to Ava and Devin. "I'm so sorry to barge in like this. I know it is such a surprise to see a ghost. Unfortunately, there is a ghost in your house that you can't see. Her name is Asia. Dear Ava, she is your heart donor."

Then Charlie took Asia by the hand and they both vanished into the crystal ball. I didn't wait for Ava or Devin to get over their shock.

"My heart donor? Wait, I need to talk to her," said Ava, almost in a panic.

"No," I said. "You don't need to talk to her right now. You need to get some rest. In the meantime, I'm going to need some help finding your heart. You've given me a lot of useful information but since we're dealing with something far more sinister than an asshole of a former boyfriend I'm going to consult with a friend of mine."

"Who? Will it cost more?" Ava asked.

"The price will stay the same. My associate, my friend, can find anything."

"Tell us about him first," said Devin.

"My friend was once tasked with finding Marie Antionette's jewels. Aren't we all. Everyone thinks there are jewels out there, but most are just rumors and wishful thinking."

"Did he find them?" Devin asked.

"Well, no," I said, "but he did find a box of trinkets that belonged to the headless queen. There were a few ribbons, a child's ring, a lock of hair from a lover along with a poorly written but extremely explicit love letter, and a few more milder love letters, and small items such as buttons, and a collection of tiny ceramic animals. There was also a vial full of brownish gray water."

"No jewels?"

"Of course not."

"So nothing," said Devin. "What was in the vial? Was it Marie Antionette's tears?"

"It wasn't tears," I said.

"What was in the vial then?" Devin asked impatiently.

"Marie Antionette's soul," I told him.

The was a hush in the room as it something had sucked all of the air out of it.

"Her soul? That's ridiculous," said Devin.

"Not any more ridiculous than Ava's heart vanishing into thin air as she lay on the operating table with her skin peeled back ready to have her chest cavity cracked open."

Devin downed the rest of his beer and stood up. "Sorry, I'm having a hard time processing all of this. It's bad enough that Eva needs a heart transplant, but...I don't know..." His eyes watered up and he wiped his eyes with the back of his hand.

"What happened to the vial?" Eva asked.

"I don't know," I said. "What I do know is that he never opened it, and that it is in a safe place."

After finishing up with Ava and Devin I went home. With Charlie's help I did some research on everything I had so far. I consulted with my crystal ball, made a few phone calls, and did a little research on both the Internet and the Dark Web. Then with Charlie and Asia tucked away in my purse (in the crystal ball of course) I headed out to the home of the one person who could help me solve this mystery of the missing heart.

* * *

After changing into something nice, grabbing a change of clothes for the next day, and a packing couple of good bottles of wine from my cellar, I headed up the road to see my friend, and treasure hunter extraordinaire, Fortunato Alexander Flannigan Orlando Rogers. Don't laugh. Guys like him rock the long names. Before I left I did a quick spell on the parameter of my house to keep out any intruders. I never know when I'm working on a case like this what might happen when I'm gone. I also brought along Maisey, my twelve year old Golden Retriever.

As I wound up the narrow road into the hills above Los Angeles Charlie had jumped out of my crystal ball and sat in the passenger seat. Maisey sat in the back with her head out the window.

"This is a tough one, even for Fortunato," said Charlie. "It would make a great movie."

"If you weren't a ghost you could star in it," I said.

"Write, produce, and direct it too," said Charlie. Then he let out a big sigh and looked out the window.

We arrived at a house that was a marvel of Arts and Crafts design with a view of the valley and the ocean to the west, and the mountains to the east. As far as I was concerned, and for many more reasons than the design, it was a bit of Heaven on Earth.

The front door opened with a flood of light into the dark night. A man of average height, but uncommon charisma greeted us.

Fortunato kissed me on the cheek, then nodded to Charlie. Maisey wiggled her rump as our host gave her a treat.

Dinner was on the grill out on the deck by the infinity pool. A red tailed hawk flew up and landed on the Catalina tile table next to me. "Hello Aurora," I said to the bird and stroked her feathers. She was Fortunato's familiar, the finder of lost dreams, and the finder of the occasional rabbit.

As we dined on steaks, grilled vegetables and a wonderful California Zinfandel, I told Fortunato everything I knew about Ava's heart.

He listened without interruption.

"Tell me more about Ava," Fortunato said as he leaned back and took a sip of his wine. "What does she do for a living?"

"Ava works for the city. She is in charge of coordinating and implementing improvements and programs to help the city withstand natural disasters. She also helps develop planning and housing policy in the office of economic development. In her spare time she runs a couple of community gardens. That includes outreach to marginalized populations, and programs for senior citizens. Her fiancé Devin is a High School English teacher. He runs creative writing programs for the teens and helps then get published in his spare time. He also volunteers at a cat shelter. That's where the cat Mr. Darcy came from."

"They sound like a socially responsible young couple. I'm impressed. Does Ava have any enemies?"

"No. Or at least none that I could find. I checked up on Devin as well. He's a good guy. Their families are also just nice regular people."

"Any paranormal connections?"

"None."

"I haven't seen you for a few weeks. How are you?"

"Fine I guess. I've been going to the dog beach a lot with Maisey."

"Sound like fun. I need to join you sometime."

"That would be great. I've been getting a lot of business lately from Reality TV stars. Most of them might as well have sold their souls already, but I'm doing my best to keeping it real for them. Anyway, it more than pays the bills."

"Are you seeing anyone?"

"Not really. You?"

He smiled. "No, I'm not."

* * *

Later that night I woke up alone. Fortunato's side of the bed was still warm. The last thing I remembers was falling asleep with his arms and legs wrapped around me and head against my shoulder. I slipped one of his robes and went out to the den where he often works.

I could see him at the table, in front of a large window with the view of a full moon and the city lights down below. Three cups were in front of him. He had the cards spread out on the table.

"I woke up with a weird feeling about some of the things you'd told me," he said. "Have a seat."

"Did you discover anything?"

"I keep getting an overwhelming sense of love from both Ava and her heart donor, as well as Devin. The vibes off of Jon Blanken were not so good. In fact they were disturbing."

"How so?"

"Look at the cups."

All three cups were filled with red liquid. Blood.

"Oh no."

"Ava got herself tangled up with a Vampire."

"Did he take her heart? Why?"

"I don't know yet. There is also a question of what happened the night Asia, the heart donor died. She comes up as nothing but trouble. She never had any jail time but has come close."

"What for?"

"Fights, disruptive public behavior, stalking, and an assortment of other general asshole stuff. Our girl Asia has annoyed just about everyone she has ever met."

"Maybe we need to talk to her."

"I was thinking the same thing."

I got out my crystal ball and summoned her out of it. Charlie also came out.

Asia appeared in a black party dress with a huge wildly colored scarf. Her long dark hair was curled and still messy from her wild dancing the night she died. For someone who was such a social outcast she was surprisingly pretty. Then again so were my Reality TV clients, but come to think of it they had the help of plastic surgery. Asia came by it naturally.

Asia looked around. "Hey, wow, this is a nice place. Look at that view."

"Asia," I said, "This is Fortunato. He is going to help me find your heart."

"Cool," she said. Then she winked at me. "He's cute. You doing the nasty with him?"

I just gave her a slight smile. Charlie snorted and put his hand over his mouth to keep from laughing.

Asia kept talking. "So do you guys have any clues yet? I mean, you're sort of like paranormal investigators or something like that."

"Something like that," said Fortunato. I believe something other than human has taken your heart Asia. That is the reason your soul is still locked here in the mortal world."

"You gotta be effing kidding me. Even now I can't get a break. I should have known something like this would have happened. Paranormal my ass. This is para-abnormal," said Asia.

"If it isn't too painful for you Asia, please tell us about the night you died," said Fortunato.

Asia sat her ghostly form down in a chair and wrapper her garish shawl around her shoulders and arms. "It isn't painful at all. I mean, it was at the time, but not now. My boyfriend Quinn and I went to Raven Nest. It's a brewpub. One of our regular places. *Was* one of our regular places. A band I like, Tumble Buns, was playing. Have you heard of Tumble Buns?"

Charlie, Fortunato, and I all said no.

"They're great. Sort of a Rock-a-Billy Emo band. Anyway, as soon as we get there, Quinn ditches me. When I find Quinn he says it is over. He broke up with me right there in front of everyone. What the crap? We just got there.

I ask him why. He tells me I have no redeemable qualities. I asked him to explain. He says first off that I eat his food. So I steal a fry or onion ring from time to time. So what? Everybody does it. Then he says I dress funny. I have a unique style. I'm artistic and a free spirit. Then he says I talk too much. So, I tell him I have a lot to say. Then he says I'm boring in bed because he can't get me to, well, you know, see fireworks. That isn't my fault. I told him he doesn't know what he is doing. It isn't my fault.

I tried to talk to him, but he called me a self-centered selfish freak. Self-centered? Selfish? I only thought of HIM. It was always about HIM. I can't believe how mean Quinn was to me that night. We'd been together for, what, six months? Yeah, six months. Almost seven.

After that I went out on the dance floor and danced by myself. I didn't care who was looking at me. Some girl called me a freak and asked me if I was on drugs. All I did was accidently brush her arm with my scarf. I wasn't even drunk. Some people are so mean. I called her a bitch and told her boyfriend that I bet she faked it when they screwed. Then Mr. Bitch's Boyfriend starts yelling at me. And no, I didn't respond. By then everyone was looking at me so I went to the bar and found a place next to Quinn. He told me I was the worst person in the world and that I was an embarrassment and left.

No sooner had I sat down on his stool I heard POW POW POW. Some asshole was standing right there with a gun, you know one of those big black automatic things that looks like it is out of some military movie. A couple next to me froze like rabbits. Awww man. I put my arms around them and another chick and got them down on the floor under the bar. I told them they'd be ok and not to be scared. And that was it. The guy shot the top of my head off. Just like that. KABAM. SPLAT. DONE.

Then Quinn has the nerve to blubber like a baby in front of the news cameras because his girlfriend Asia, a true hero, had died. Fuck him."

"You saved three people."

"Better them than me. Really. I know I'm weird. I know I say stupid things. Nobody gives a crap about me. The people I save were normal. They didn't deserve to die."

"You didn't deserve to die either."

"I guess, maybe, maybe not, but I saved more than three people. There were three at the bar. Then, because I was an organ donor, my eyes went to someone, my kidneys, my liver. Even my face.

Yeah, I donated my face. I'm pretty weird, but I'm also pretty pretty if you know what I mean. A sweet woman who had her face blown off by some dirt bag ex-boyfriend got my pretty face. How cool is that? She'll be able to have a normal life again. I never had a normal life, but now she can with my face. With MY face.

But my heart. Someone took my heart and now... You know, after I died, everyone else who died and I sort of traveled down this path toward a light. It was like hiking through the redwoods, but I've never been to see the redwoods because nobody would ever go with me. Then I was back here. Poof. Just like that. I want to go down that redwood path again. You have to find my heart and give it to Ava. She needs my heart. I want her to have it. She deserves it. I want to go back to the redwoods."

Then Asia gave us an especially serious look furrowing her pretty ghost brows. "Asia. Ava. Our names even sound sort of alike. It was meant to be. I didn't do shit when I was alive. Now that I can make a difference, son of a bitch, nothing ever goes right for me, even when I do the right thing."

"Shhhhhh. We'll find your heart Asia," I said.

"God damn Quinn. He's the kind of guy who eats bubble gum flavored ice cream. No adult should eat bubble gum ice cream. It should have been the top his head that was blown off."

"Would Quinn want your heart Asia?" Fortunato asked her.

"Hell no. He already has a new boring vanilla regular normal girlfriend. It's freaking pathetic. Holy crap, my death is the best thing that ever happened to him."

I didn't tell Asia that I'd already contacted Quinn. He was a nice normal guy. He had been devastated by what happened to Asia.

"Asia was kind of a lost soul, but she had a good heart. I remember when she put the donor designation on her driver's license. She was so proud. A month later she was dead."

"Do you know who might have taken her heart?" I asked.

"No," said Quinn said, as he wiped away a tear with the back of his hand.

I had Charlie take Asia back into the crystal ball. She'd just get into more trouble if she was allowed to ramble around in Fortunato's home. Plus I'd know where she was if I needed more information from her.

Right now our most important task was finding Jon Blanken. Actually the most important task was getting a few hours more sleep, and maybe, well, some more quality personal time with Fortunato.

* * *

As the sun came up in the morning I kicked the ghosts out of my crystal ball and got to work searching for Jon Blanken. Fortunato was out on his deck meditating and hopefully getting some messages from wherever he gets his messages.

After about twenty minutes he came inside. "Have you had coffee yet? I'm making some."

Over coffee, fruit, and some exceptionally good bagels, he told me he'd found Jon Blanken. The coward had burned down his house and escaped to one of his other properties in Palm Springs.

We left Maisey at the house with Charles and Asia and took off for a visit with Blanken. The drive was a little over two hours. I might be a Witch but I don't ride a broom. We took Fortunato's hybrid SUV and talked along the way.

It was also so comfortable and familiar between us. For over fifty years we'd worked together, become friend, then become more than friends. For all of the time I'd known him there was still something mysterious about him. He was incredibly spiritual and kind, but at the same time he was one of the most savage beings I'd ever met. I still didn't know quite how old he was or where he had come from. The answers were always vague and hidden away in dark places even I didn't dare go. He was whatever he needed to be, which was fine with me.

We arrived at a modern atomic age glass structure surrounded by century plants and barrel cactus planted in tan colored rocks.

"Nice house," I said.

"I guess, if you like that kind of thing," said Fortunato.

There was no need to knock. I spouted off a spell and blew the door off of its hinges.

Blanken was sitting on the couch binge watching *Somebody Feed Phil* on Netflix. He sat stunned as we entered in a cloud of blue smoke (my own special touch.)

"Who the hell are you?" the Vampire Blanken asked.

"Where is Ava's heart?" Fortunato asked as he walked up to Blanken.

"I don't know what you're talking about," said Blanken.

Fortunato grabbed Blanken by the neck and lifted him about six inches off of the ground. "Where is Ava's heart?"

"I don't have it," Blanken hissed out.

"Tell us what you did with it then," said Fortunato as he tightened his grip, then dropped the Vampire to the floor. Blanken hissed showing his fangs.

Fortunato laughed at him. "You're such a pathetic little rat. Where is Ava's heart?"

"You don't understand," whined Blanken. "I was turning her. I was taking it slow."

"Turning her? As in turning Ava into a Vampire?" I said shocked by the revelation.

"Yes, do I have to spell it out? I was turning her into a Vampire. She didn't know. When she left me I was half way through. It damaged her heart."

"She didn't know? That is unacceptable even for the worst of Vampires. You're nothing but an opportunistic ghoul," I said.

"You destroyed her heart," said Fortunato. "Why didn't you go after her and finish it?"

Jon Blanken started to fidget and his bottom lip started to quiver. "You don't know Ava. She's strong. I've never met a woman who was so strong. I couldn't keep her. She turned me away."

"The you stole the heart that was going to replace the one *you* damaged," said Fortunato.

"It wasn't like that," snapped Blanken.

"Then tell me what it was like Blanken? What did you do with the heart?"

"I sold it."

"Why?"

"Because if Ava had a new heart she'd never take me back. I'd never be able to turn her into a Vampire."

"Ava's heart is beyond repair by your inept attempts. You will never be able to turn her into a Vampire you idiot," said Fortunato.

"Who did you sell it to?" I asked.

"The Demon Goblin Queen. She is auctioning it off tonight to the highest bidder."

"Oh shit," I said. "Fortunato, we'd better get going."

* * *

I called Ava and updated her on the situation. Devin insisted on going along with us. I tried to talk him out of it, but finally Fortunato agreed to have him along.

We arrived just in time to the auction house of The Demon Goblin Queen, Belinda Bozella. The last time I was here was when I purchased a vat of dried elf skin I needed for some rather difficult spells. That must have been at least thirty years ago.

The auction house was crowded with just a few seats left in the back. Devin looked around at the crowd no doubt wondering what horror film he'd just walked into.

Belinda Bozella stood at the auction block, all tightly wrapped in a silver and black wiggle dress, with red hair piled about three feet above her head. Then with a brief introduction she started the bidding. "One human heart. Belonged to a twenty six year old female human. A heart taken from the operating table as it waited to be transplanted into the chest of another. What will you give for it."

The would be buyers called out their offers.

"Joaquim Murrieta's Head," called out a man in a green plaid jacket.

"Adolph Hitler's Dirty Underwear," yelled a demon.

"The skull of a nun," another screamed out. "A nun who killed twenty children and a priest."

"Twenty million dollars," said someone in the front row.

"A load of unicorn manure," a woman yelled out.

"My heart. You can take my heart in exchange for Asia's heart," rang out a voice so sweet and pure that half of the crowd winced in pain.

"No, Devin. No" I said.

"Retract that bid," called out Fortunato.

Belinda shook her head. "There are no retractions allowed, unless of course…" She smiled a smile full of sharp white teeth. "You would like to give me Isolde's dog Maisey."

"No. Absolutely not," said Devin.

Belinda squinted at Devin. "Who are you?"

"He's a high school English teacher. He teaches AP English and creative writing. His heart is useless to you," said Fortunato.

"Why do you want this heart English teacher?" Belinda asked.

Devin stood up and answered. "It was supposed to go to the woman I love. It was stolen off of the operating table by the Vampire Jon Blanken."

"I see," said Belinda.

"No, you don't see," said Devin. "She needs this heart."

Fortunato stood up next to him. "Devin please, stop talking. Belinda, his heart is no use to you. The man is just a normal guy. There is no magic in him."

"There is no magic in the heart he wishes to purchase either," said Belinda.

My purse jolted and Asia jumped out of the crystal ball. "Excuse me. That was my heart you're talking about bitch. There is plenty of magic in it. Go fuck yourself and give the English teacher MY HEART."

Belinda looked annoyed. "You're a ghost. What do you care?"

"Blow me," snapped Asia.

Belinda's face became a mask of anger. "One more word and you will be removed permanently, and young lady I mean permanently as in forever. Does anyone else wish to bid?"

"The propeller of Amelia Earhart's plane," yelled someone with a horn coming out of his forehead.

"Jeffrey Dahmer's teeth!" yelled a bony vampire in a black and red Halston halter dress.

"Cromwell's Head," yelled a man with a long white beard.

"No, I don't need any more heads," yelled Belinda.

"Mata Hari's head," yelled a man in a white suit standing in the back.

"I said no more heads," roared Belinda.

"The Oak Island Treasure," cried someone from the middle.

Belinda rolled her eyes. "Oh please. Don't waste my time."

The she scanned the crowd and yelled, "The heart of the woman loved by the poor pathetic High School English teacher. Going once, going twice."

"Marie Antionette's Soul," a voice rang out strong and clear.

Belinda looked shocked. "Fortunato, you have Marie Antionette's soul?"

"Yes, I do," he said.

Belinda smiled. "Really?"

"Would I lie to you Belinda?"

"You'd part with it for this common heart?"

"It's not common," yelled Asia.

"Asia, hush," I hissed at her.

"Yes, the heart is more valuable to me than the soul of a headless queen. I'll throw in a petrified piece of cake and a couple of extremely dirty love letters to sweeten the deal," said Fortunato.

"What else?" Belinda asked.

"A kiss," said Fortunato.

Belinda smiled, "From you?"

"From me."

Belinda slammed her gavel down. "Sold to Fortunato Rogers."

A resounding cheer went up.

* * *

The following morning Asia's heart was put into Ava's chest where it began to beat strong and steady.

Asia kissed Charlie and took a walk along the redwood path toward the light.

I went back to my house by the beach with Charlie and Maisey. That afternoon I had a Zoom call with the California Witch's Alliance. After taking care of some paperwork and taking a long shower I sat on a chair in my backyard and tried to clear my brain.

The love that Devin had for Ava blew me over. It was something that might seem so rare to some, but was it really? Who wouldn't give their heart to save the person they love the most? Then I thought about Asia and how she threw herself over three strangers to save them and didn't even seem to care that she died. Her happiness came from somewhere in a deep place that we all have, but rarely even know it exists.

Then I thought about Fortunato. That was a bad idea. He was brilliant, and sexy, and scary, and a total mystery, and if I kept this up I was going to end up with a damaged heart.

Then I heard a familiar voice say my name.

"Isolde."

I turned to see Fortunato standing there.

"Hello. I didn't expect to see you," I said.

He smiled. "We have some unfinished business Isolde."

"Well," I said, "I hope you've rinsed your mouth out and wiped all of the Goblin spit off of your lips."

Fortunato smiled at me and laughed.

Like a good Witch I was ready for the night. Ready to solve another mystery. And now, ready to believe in love.

Deviant Shadows

CHARLIE
By Dave Henderson

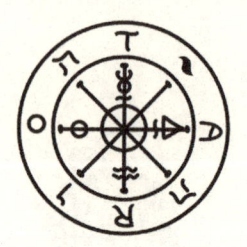

Charlie is my best friend. We've known each other for 12 years. We met back when I was homeless.

Life throws you some shit sometimes. Had lost my job, got divorced, you know… same old horrorshow.

I had set up a shelter of sorts, using cardboard and some trash bags. Kept most of the rain off. I had a pay-as-you-go cellphone, and had been using that and the library computers trying to find a gig. I write software. Figured I could maybe find something to get by until I can get my laptop out of hock.

I was looking through job listings on the phone, when something hit me on the head, and scared the hell out of me. It was a plastic bag, like you get from the corner store. Two cans of tuna rolled out, and a long box of a single sleeve of saltines poked out of the bag.

I looked up, and there was a big black cat. He stared at me a minute, and then jumped down from the top of my box.

He meaowed once, as if apologizing, and then rubbed up along side me. Then he sat down by the tuna, and stared at me.

He was a handsome fellow. Solid glossy black, with a blaze of white on his chest. It was kinda odd looking. Reminded me of that Halloween cartoon, where Charlie was in his shitty ghost costume, and only got a rock. There were even two little tufts of black for the eyes.

"Well there, I am guessing you need me to open those cans, yeah?"

He meaowed again, letting me know that 'Yes, that is indeed what I need.'

I opened a can, and set it down in front of him. He sniffed at it, and then pawed the other can over to me.

"Two at once? Sheesh. Greedy, aren't you?" I popped that one open and set it down. He gave out a frustrated sneeze, and pushed that can back over by the bag and the saltines. Then he meaowed once and stared at me.

"Oh! This is for me? Well thanks, buddy." As soon as I started eating, he gave another sneeze, and we had lunch together.

We finished at about the same time. I poured him some water from my bottle, once I rinsed my can out. He thought that was a great idea.

"Well, thank you for lunch! My name is Seth. Ok if I call you Charlie? You remind me of someone."

He paused in his face wash, looked me in the eye, and gave another sneeze, which was cat for 'Yes, I find that acceptable.'

He curled up beside me for a while, as I went back to job hunting. After about an hour, he got up, stretched, yawned, and gave me a head butt. Then he started walking away down the alley.

"Come back soon, Charlie!"

He stopped, and looked back and meaowed, and went on his way.

* * *

I was asleep in my shelter that night, when Charlie came back. He purred and bumped at my face until I woke up.

"Hey, Charlie. Welcome back! Mi casa es su casa, such as it is." He thought that was a fine idea, and curled up next to me. It was the best sleep I had had in the box.

The next morning, I was headed off to the nearby church that served breakfast to the homeless.

"I need coffee and eggs, Charlie. You can come along, but you will need to stay outside." He gave a sneeze, and off we went.

* * *

I came back out, paper cup of coffee in hand, and was pleasantly surprised to see Charlie still waiting for me. He was playing with a wadded up flyer of some kind.

He stopped and gave me a stare. Then he bopped his toy over to me. I bent over to pick it up, and just for curiosity, spread it out.

It was for an agency that helps homeless people get a place to live. Nothing fancy, just efficiency digs. Have to be drug and alcohol free, but I have that covered.

"Damn, Charlie! This is great! I'm going to give them a call right now!"

Charlie gave a sneeze, rubbed around my feet, and headed off.

"I'll see you tonight at our box, yeah?"

He looked back and meaowed, and went on his way. A cat with business to be done.

* * *

It took about two weeks to get a place. No pets allowed, but I left the window open at night just enough so Charlie could get in and out.

Things were really looking up. I got a job at a small grocery, stocking, washing floors… that kind of thing. Got my laptop out of hock. Eventually, landed a programming gig that was all remote. Once that paycheck hit, we were able to move to a real apartment. And Charlie always had his daily schedule to get to.

* * *

The programming job turned into a real life saver. It took some years, but now I was the lead for a team. We had 'moved on up' to a condo, on the fifth floor of a secure building. They had 24 hour doormen. Didn't see the night guy much, but got to be good friends with the day man. His name was Tony.

Charlie still has his daytime rounds to make. No idea what he does all day, but he always comes back.

He'd want to head out after breakfast, always with a meaow as he left. At first I'd walk him down to the ground floor, and kind of sneak him out the service entrance. Tony figured that out pretty quickly.

"Seth, you can let him out the front door." So, the next morning, Charlie said 'Goodbye' and off through the front door he went, a fashionable cat-about-town.

He'd always come back just before Tony went off shift. Tony would let him in, and they would visit at his desk until I came down.

"I dunno, Seth. Fine lookin' fella like this. I bet he's got a string of ladies to visit every day."

"Is that it, Charlie? You a heartbreaker?" Charlie looked back and forth at us from his place on Tony's desk, and sneezed. Not sure if that was yes or no, but he was definite about it, either way.

* * *

Then one night, Charlie was late. Tony called me from the lobby.

"Our man ain't home yet, Seth. I am on my way out, but Bill the night man will keep an eye out."

"Thanks, Tony. I'm sure he'll show up soon."

Five minutes later, Tony called back. "Seth, you need to come down right away." His voice sounded thick.

"What's up, Tony?"

"Just get down here."

I walked out of the elevator to see Tony and Bill bent over a box on the desk. Tony looked up, tears in his eyes.

"I am so sorry, Seth."

In the box was Charlie. He looked like he had been mauled.

"Fuck! Charlie!"

Charlie meaowed once quietly, and stared into my eyes.

"I found him in the alley as I was on the way to my car. I'd have missed him, but he called me."

There was a 24 emergency vet about 8 blocks away. Tony drove us there.

"You gonna be ok, Seth? You need me to stay?"

"No. Thanks Tony, but I will be staying here until Charlie comes home, or they kick me out."

We went in, and they took him to clean him up and evaluate. I sat there in the lobby.

The pretty young lady at the front desk offered me coffee or water, and said, "Dr. Daminis is the best vet in the Tri-State, Mr. Robinson. Charlie is in good hands."

"Thanks. I appreciate it."

The vet came out to the lobby. "Let's go see Charlie, Seth."

We walked back to one of the little cubical rooms down the hall. Charlie was swaddled up and bandaged. Stitches closed the gashes. He looked up at me and sneezed.

"Glad to see you, too, Charlie. Thanks for fixing him up, Doc."

The doctor had a grim look, and put a warm, friendly hand on my shoulder. "I'm sorry, Seth. The internal damage is too much. Charlie is not going to survive this. I am so sorry."

He caught me when my knees folded, and helped me into a chair.

"He is sedated, and not in pain. You two take all the time you need, and just hit the call button by the door when you are ready or if you need anything else. Again, I am so sorry. I did all I could."

He left us, and at first we just sat there. I rubbed on his head, careful to not disturb any of the bandaging or stitches.

"Damn, Charlie. Why couldn't you just be a goddamn house cat?"

Charlie looked in my eyes. He meaowed. He was telling me something. I had no idea what it was, but he wanted me to know, whatever it was. He meaowed again, still staring at me.

"Ok, Charlie. I got you. I promise."

He gave a sneeze. He agreed. Then he closed his eyes, and they never opened back up.

* * *

The vet's office promised they would take care of Charlie for me, and would call when I could pick up his ashes. It was raining when I walked out. I walked the eight blocks home. Bill let me in, and offered condolences when I told what happened. He gave me Tony's home phone number, and I called him.

"Dammit. I am really sorry, Seth. You need an ear? Maybe a drink? I can swing by, no problem."

"Thanks, man. Maybe later. I need to be alone right now."

* * *

Somehow I fell asleep. Woke up bleary and stared at my coffee. I emailed work, explained the situation and that I had to take care of this today. My boss sent me a very nice email back, and she said to take all the time I needed. She was a cat person, too.

Like a robot, I made breakfast, drank my coffee, and read the news online.

It wasn't a top headline, but it was one of the trending stories recommended to me:

Hero Cat Saves Young Child
by Christie Aaravind

HOUSTON, Texas – A 5-year-old girl is safe today, after a feral dog attack was thwarted by a hero cat, Harris County Sheriff's Office says.

Kimberley Castillo (5) was attacked by a feral dog in Addison Park, shortly after 8 am yesterday.

Her father, Ralph Santini described what happened.

"We were just walking through the park. I bent down to tie my shoe, and Kim kept walking. I was just standing back up, and that dog grabbed her sleeve."

Her father continued, "I started running to her, and this big black cat launched it self right up on the dog's head. Latched onto an ear, and started tearing the dog's head and face up. The dog let Kim go, and I picked her up."

Bystander Katja Gevorgyan caught the following video from her cell phone.

<VIDEO LINK>

She explained, "I heard this growling and hissing and spitting, and the little girl screaming. I turned around, and saw the dog let the girl go. I already had my phone in hand, so I started recording. Those two took off into the woods, and I lost them after that."

Mr. Santini added, "I hope they find that cat. I will personally give him his own salmon."

Harris County Sheriff's Office reports that the dog was located and has been euthanized as a dangerous animal. The cat has not been found at this time.

If you have any information about this cat, please contact caaravind@httimes (dot) com.

COMMENTS (1635)

User1356: I know that cat. He comes by the senior center almost every day. I hope he is ok. He's a real lovebug.

User99654: my kid says this cat comes to her school sometimes and visits with the kids.

User34267: that cat saved my life, too. I was in a bad place. I had bought a coffee, and dosed it up with what was going to end it all. I set it down on the bench to write my goodbyes. That cat jumped up on the bench, looked me in the eye, and tossed that cup off the bench. Then he sat down next to me. I ended up calling that 800 suicide line. Thanks, buddy. I hope you are ok.

* * *

The comments kept growing. Charlie wasn't just my cat. He touched hundreds and hundreds of people. That was what he did all day. That was why he helped me. That was what he was trying to tell me.

"Goddamn it Charlie… you just had to be a hero, didn't you? That's who you were."

And I cried, not just for Charlie, but for all the others who had lost him, too.

* * *

That afternoon the vet's office called. Charlie was ready for me to pick up. I washed up, shaved, put on my best shirt, and polished up my boots. No sloppy bum for Charlie.

They had him in a nice urn. The vet and the receptionist had seen the news and the video. The urn said 'Charlie - A Real Hero'.

"Wow... I don't know what to say. Thank you very much." Then the tears again.

The receptionist gave me a hug. "It was our pleasure. Charlie was very special."

* * *

It was raining again. I put Charlie in a plastic bag, and decided to walk home. The rain matched my mood. I got back home, visited with Tony, who had also seen the news. He got choked up when he saw the engraving.

"Yeah, a big damn hero, our boy."

I put Charlie on the mantelpiece. I don't usually drink, but I keep some vodka in the freezer. I was pouring a shot, and I heard it.

"Meaow" and a sneeze. I dropped the bottle, and it glugged out over the counter. Again, "Meaow" and a sneeze. It sounded like it was out in the hall. I left the mess and opened my door.

No one in the hall.

"Meaow" and a sneeze, but sounding like it was in the staircase.

I followed the stairs all the way down to the lobby. Tony saw me.

"You ok, Seth?"

"Meaow" and a sneeze... sounding like it was outside the front door.

"Did you hear that, Tony? Tell me you heard that!"

"Heard what? You sure you are ok?"

I went outside. The rain had stopped.

"Meaow" and a sneeze, this time from the alley.

I left Tony gaping at me, and ran to the alley.

"Meaow" and a sneeze, from the dumpster down the alley.

"God dammit, whoever you are, I am going to tear you a new asshole!"

I got down to the dumpster. I didn't see anyone. I did see a small cardboard box, soaked from the rain. I bent down to look at it, and "Meaow" and a sneeze, from above me.

"Charlie? " He was sitting there on the dumpster lid. He was kind of hazy, like when you watch those holograms of dead artists performing. "What is it you want, buddy? Please… what are you trying to tell me?"

He looked at the box.

"Ok, Charlie… ok." I opened it up and there were three tiny kittens, eyes not even open yet.

"Oh, you poor little buggers."

Charlie let out a sneeze.

"I'm taking them to the vet's now, Charlie. Will you be here when I get back?"

Charlie jumped down, and even though I couldn't feel it, he rubbed himself around my legs, purring. Then he walked down the alley, fading away with a final meaow.

A True Story
By L.A. Guettler

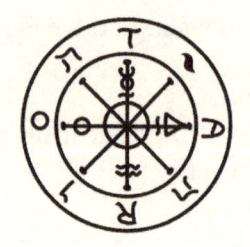

Once upon a time, there was a magical fairy princess and one day the cutest and most popular prince in the whole kingdom asked her to a party and they lived happily ever after.

Okay, so, surprise! This is a true story. The princess is me, Carrie Michaels, and the prince is Zack Garber. I mean, I'm not a princess, I'm a freshman, and it's not a kingdom, it's just Claremont High School. Zack isn't a prince but he is the cutest and most popular guy in the whole school, so he might as well be. Still, that part's not exactly true. And I'm not sure about the "happily ever after" part. So I guess it's not, like, one hundred percent a true story. I think it's super important to only tell the absolute truth, don't you?

Anyway, there is one other part of this story that's totally true: Zack asked me out! Me! Carrie! I didn't even know he knew I existed, you know? But then today I was just standing at my locker looking for my Spanish book when he just kind of comes up to me with this adorable dopey smile and asks if I want to go with him to Becca's party on Friday. "It's okay if you're busy and can't go," he said. Ha! Like I'm ever busy. I think I was in shock or something cuz I just stood there like a total idiot. I mean, he's ZACK GARBER. I must've nodded cuz he said, "Cool, I'll pick you up at 8." Then he walked back to his friends and Brad gave him a fist bump.

So…I don't want to be, like, reading too much into stuff? But it looked like that fist bump thing was Brad congratulating Zack, which could maybe mean Zack likes me. I mean, he could ask any girl in the whole school to go to Becca's party and they'd say yes. Who could say no to Zack Garber?

* * *

I can't believe she fell for it. The stupid bitch actually fell for it. You should've seen her. I didn't think her face could look any dumber, but there it was, mouth hanging open and eyes all bugged out. I think she drooled a little. I'm gonna kill Brad for this. He thinks that just because I lost that stupid bet means he can ruin my life. How was I supposed to know he could sink so many three-pointers in a row? The dude can barely dribble. I still think it was some kind of scam.

This is my senior year, goddamnit. It's supposed to be the best year of my whole life until college, and I'm stuck going to Becca's big end-of-the-year party with a freshman. And not even one of the good freshmen, like Lindsey Hollings. That girl's hot as hell. No, I get a certified pizza face with no tits. I'm not even sure what her name is, I think it's Carly? She's in my gym class. Not something you'd want to see doing burpees, let me tell you.

I was really, really hoping she'd say no. But Brad was right. He didn't have to rub it in, though. The fist bump was a dick move. I mean, she's got to know there's no way I'm actually interested in her, right? I could have any girl in whole school. Who'd say no?

* * *

This is it! My big date with Zack is tonight and I'm so excited I might, like, have a stroke. I spent all week trying to figure out what to wear but all my clothes are boring. All I've got is this dress from eighth grade graduation but this is ZACK GARBER and you don't just wear an old junior high dress to a high school party with a bunch of seniors. So now I've got the cutest outfit. The skirt's really short but who cares? I hope Zack likes it. He's supposed to be here to pick me up any minute. I'm so nervous I'm sweating, but I know it'll be awesome if I can just keep myself from dorking out too much.

Oh my god, he's here.

* * *

Oh my god, what is she even wearing? And why is she all sweaty? Jesus. Okay, I just need to get to the party and let Brad see us, then I can ditch her and hopefully salvage the night. Maybe Lindsey will be there.

So she gets in the car and I'm like, "Hey, Carly." But it turns out her name is actually Carrie. Like it matters? She started rambling on about her new skirt so I snuck a peek just to see what she's blabbering about. Her legs are pretty good, actually. Not great, of course. But considering the rest, pretty good.

She won't shut up about the dumb skirt and now it's all I can think about. That and her panties. I wonder if they're new, too. I'm kinda grossed out by the whole thing. Like I said, she's no Lindsey. But she might be fun. I bet she's completely untouched. Not like the stuck-up bitches in my class. You really gotta work at them just to get a little taste, even though you know they've been on their knees for every guy in the school and half the teachers too. This girl, though, she'd probably be so grateful for the attention that she'd do just about anything. I bet I could get in her back door. If I wanted to. I kind of want to.

* * *

Zack is really different when he's not in school. Like, usually he's really funny and laughing all the time, but now he's just kind of quiet. Maybe it's my fault for making him feel bad about getting my name wrong. It's not a big deal, I know, it's just a name and Carly's a lot cooler name than Carrie anyway. I probably should've just let it go. He gave me kind of a nasty look, even though I tried really hard to be nice about it and make it like a joke. So I told him all about skirt and stuff, which I think helped a lot! He keeps looking at me, like out of the corner of his eye, the whole time he's driving. I hope he's paying attention to where he's going. I've never been to Becca's house, but I'm pretty sure he's going the wrong way. There's nothing up this way but the woods. I mean, I like the woods and all, but it's awfully dark.

* * *

I'm going for it. Maybe if I run into Lindsey later, I can make it a double header.

* * *

Ugh! Zack Garber is not a prince AT ALL, he's a total jerk, and that's the absolute truth. He pulled off the road onto this, like, dirt track or something and stupid me, I thought the was just going to turn around, like "ha ha, I guess I got lost." But no, suddenly he's rubbing my leg and asking about my underwear. At first it was kind of funny, I guess, but he wouldn't stop. I tried telling him we'd be late for the party, that Becca would be wondering why he wasn't there, that Brad was probably drinking all the beer and we didn't want to miss out. None of it did any good, he just pushed up my skirt. I said NO, like really loud, but I think that just made him kinda mad cuz he got sort of rough, doing stuff with his fingers. I started to cry and he got REALLY mad this time and punched me. Not hard cuz we were in the car still and he couldn't get a good angle or whatever, but still, it really hurt. Somehow I got the door open and fell out onto the dirt. I think my skirt got torn.

Anyway, I got up and ran. But not too fast.

* * *

Stupid goddamn bitch, who the fuck does she think she is? She's a freshman, she's no one. Fuck. Now she's off in the woods someplace and I'm left with this raging hardon. I don't get left with raging hardons. I'm captain of the basketball team. I'm going to be fucking PROM KING. Every girl wants my dick. I've been sucked off by 15 different girls just this year. This one, Carrie or whatever, she wanted it too. She could say no all day long but of course she fucking wanted it. This was her golden opportunity to be someone at this school. I bet she bought that skirt on purpose just to trick me into doing something so she could be part of the Zack Garber Club but then she fucking chickened out. Now I bet she's thinking she'll tell everyone I couldn't get it up or something. Make it seem like my fault.

Well, I'll show her. That cockteasing bitch will be real fucking sorry when I catch her. And I will catch her. The dumb cunt must've had a glow stick or something, cuz there's this green light bouncing around in the trees. It's like she wants me to catch her.

* * *

So, like, remember how I said the magical fairy princess was me only I'm not really a princess but the rest was totally true? I suppose that, like, technically I'm not a magical fairy either.

* * *

It's so weird, she isn't heading back toward the road, and she's not even going that fast. But every time I think I'm getting close, she's gone. Well, she can't run forever. If I could just get out of these trees I'd—

* * *

But a wisp is way closer to a magical fairy than a freshman at Claremont High, right? So it's still a true story, sort of.

* * *

Fuck! Fuck fuck fuck, my leg! It's fucking broken! What is this, a well? Oh my god, oh my god. I gotta get out of here, gotta get out, holy shit, I gotta get out. Where's Carly, I mean Carrie, she'll help me, she's wouldn't let me just die here.

Wait, there's the green light again, way up there. I can't see her face but she's gotta hear me screaming, right? What's she doing just standing there? Come on, it was just a joke back there in the car. I'm a good guy, honest, you just didn't get the joke. Please, please help me, for god's sake, my leg really hurts.

* * *

Okay, if I'm completely honest? I didn't expect him to survive the fall. Just boom, quick. He wasn't supposed to feel anything, you know? Maybe I should—

* * *

I'm fucking begging you, you stupid bitch. Are you happy now? This is all your fault but I'm fucking begging you. Now get your fat ass over here and help me or I swear to fucking God when I get out of here I'll beat the shit out of you.

* * *

Never mind.

* * *

Oh my god no, I didn't mean it, I swear I didn't. I'll do whatever you want. You want an apology? I'm sorry, okay? I'm sorry! I'M SORRY. Money? I can get you money, just tell me how much and it's yours. I won't tell the cops or anything, I promise. It'll be our secret. Just—no, please, don't go!

* * *

Once upon a time, there was a magical fairy princess who wasn't a fairy princess at all, and one day the biggest asshole at Claremont High asked her to a party and she, at least, lived happily ever after.

ESSENCE
By Soleil Daniels

Forever born.
Forever die.
Stuck in between,
Says the living's eye.
Alive is dead,
And death,
Alive.
To feed upon the gift of life.
Immortal is not truth,
But lies.
To take the blood,
The sweat,
The tears,
And feed from happiness,
Their hopes,
Their fears.
To choose is not
What one should want.
Eternal is tempting,
But at the cost,
Would surely only be a loss.

Desert Winds
By Juliette Kings
aka The Vampire Maman

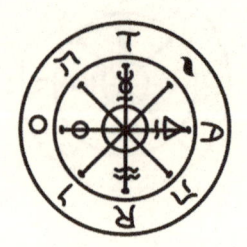

On the edge of the Sandia Mountains, my friend Amelia, her husband Raul, and I drove down the gravel road to the home of Ximena, an ancient woman who mostly lived in solitude with the company of the birds and the wind.

Ximena's home was a large old adobe structure rimmed with bells and bushes of purple flowers. She greeted us at the door, as always wearing a long, colorful skirt. Her black hair flowed down her back, almost to her knees. Dark eyes smiled at us in a welcome greeting, as did her fangs. She is as old as the mountains, yet Ximena looks like a young college girl.

We entered the main room. Walls lined with books and crystals flanked part of the room with windows on the other side looking toward the mountains. We could smell the dried chile ristras hanging in the kitchen. A red-shouldered hawk perched on a wooden chair. It called out when it saw us.

"Maria, you still sing so sweetly," I said to the bird. She gave me a cold stare, then allowed me to pet her feathered head.

Maria the hawk had been around since I was a young woman, more than a hundred years. I wondered at times how she could live so long, then I stopped wondering and chalked it up to magic, love, or pure mystery. It is what it is. That is how things work, here in the land of magic.

A youngish man with dark hair and eyes like Ximena, but pale skin, came into the room. He was introduced to us as Kyle. But he wasn't like us. I could feel his warmth as soon as he walked into the room.

Kyle was a man of many talents. He was a photographer, a teacher, a writer, an engineer and apparently a lover. After talking over wine and a light diner we also discovered Ximena's young friend was also extremely opened minded.

He was also a young widower. One night left him alone with his dreams dead, but he kept going and kept at least a portion of the dreams and spark alive.

While Raul, Amelia and Ximena went to a back room to examine some old maps or something, Kyle and I went out to the porch. Bats flew about as the sounds of the bells filled the air.

Kyle asked me about my husband, Teddy. I smiled shyly and told him how we'd met as kids and fallen in love a hundred years later. I think I'd always been in love with my husband on some level.

Then Kyle spoke of his lost love. "After Kayla, my wife, passed away, everyone kept asking me if I'd go back. Over and over they'd ask the old 'what if' question. You know, you can't go back. I can't bring her back. I will never forget her. She is part of me, but I live in the world of the living."

"No ghost?" I had to ask.

"Only a Vampire in the Southwest would ask that," Kyle answered with a knowing smile.

"A Vampire anywhere would ask that. Don't get me started on the ghosts I see all the time."

"No ghost. Kayla moved on the night she died. That is a good thing."

"Yes, it is. You're a wise man with a loving heart. In some circles that is a rare thing."

He leaned against the rail. "I don't know you except by reputation, but I want to ask you a few things, or at least see how you feel about a few things."

"Okay," I said.

"I'm in love with Ximena. I know what she is. I know how old she is. It doesn't matter."

I shrugged and laughed. "My 500 or so year old Grandmama is in love with a 35 year old. What are you, about 38?"

He smiled. I was correct. He was 38 and absolutely a delight – young, yet years ahead of most men his age.

"Dear Kyle, you also want me to tell you if I think it would be wise if you became a Vampire? Right?"

He smiled an uncomfortable hot-blooded smile.

I said to him, "Kyle, you are in love with the cold wind under the moon and the sprint of night. She is an amazing being. I've always admired her. If you feel you can make a life out here with her, then do it. But don't lose yourself in her. Always be who you are, even after you become a Vampire. That is the only way it will work. If you try to be too much like her, she will leave you, because she fell in love with you, not with herself."

Raul and Ximena came out to join us with wine for Ryan and spiced blood for the rest of us.

Ximena whistled and Maria the red-shouldered hawk came and landed on a table next to her hand. Ximena gave the bird a piece of meat she took from a bag in her pocket.

Into the night we talked until the sun came up and created unbelievably beautiful light and shadows on the mountains.

I could hear the wind whispering to the lovers:

The light
in dark eyes
promises kept
forever and
again
in our hearts
we love
we laugh
and we learn
to do it
all
over
again.

The Girl in the Mirror
By Mandy White

"This stops now."

"But Daddy! Deedee needs to eat too!"

"She's just a little girl, Hal. It's just harmless fun." Melanie's mother said.

"No more! She's getting too old for that crap! She starts school this year, and what will everyone think?"

"They'll think she's just a normal kid, just like her classmates."

"Normal kids don't act like that."

From that day forward, only one plate was placed at the table in front of Melanie. It didn't matter that Deedee wasn't allowed a plate at the dinner table; she was present nonetheless, sitting in silence at Melanie's side, sharing her plate and her meals.

Deedee had been her best friend ever since Melanie could remember. Her first memory was of learning to walk together, climbing to their feet side by side, using furniture for balance. They learned to talk, first in a language only they understood. Melanie's mother always smiled at the sound of happy chatter coming from the nursery. A happy baby was a healthy baby.

Growing up, Melanie and Deedee were inseparable. There were always two places set for tea parties on the little table in her room.

Melanie wanted a place set for Deedee at meal times. Her mother humored her at first, but when she turned five, her father put his foot down and banned Deedee from the dinner table.

The dinner place setting was just one in a long, endless string of arguments between Melanie's parents. They had been yelling at each other ever since she could remember. She stopped talking about

Deedee and stayed in her room to avoid the arguments, which was most of the time. She took comfort in Deedee's companionship. As long as they had each other, Melanie was never alone.

One day, Melanie's father left and didn't come back. She never saw her father again. Her mother said it was because of something called Divorce. Her mother also called her father "That Cheating Bastard", although Melanie never did figure out what game he cheated at. She also called him a lot of words Melanie wasn't allowed to say. With her father gone, the house felt peaceful and her mom seemed happier. Melanie kept quiet about Deedee for fear of disturbing her mother.

* * *

On the first day of school, Melanie couldn't wait to introduce Deedee to all of her new friends. Sadly, her classmates did not share her enthusiasm for Deedee. They laughed and called her a weirdo. After that first day, Deedee still came to school, but Melanie stopped talking about her to other people. She wanted to ask Deedee to stay home, but was afraid of how she would react. Deedee could be… difficult sometimes. Like the time Becky Johnson fell off the swing. Melanie was waiting for a turn, but Deedee didn't want to wait. She shoved Becky, causing her to land on her face, splitting her lip and breaking one of her teeth. Melanie was sent home for bullying and she couldn't tell anyone what had really happened.

* * *

As Melanie grew older and she made a few friends at school, Deedee's companionship became less important. In fact, she was becoming a bit of a third wheel. At age 8, she mustered the courage to tell Deedee that she didn't want her company at school anymore. Deedee didn't take the news well. She smashed everything breakable in Melanie's bedroom, beginning with the little tea set they had always played with. Melanie's mother was furious and took away her television privileges for a month. Deedee kept quiet after that, but Melanie still sensed her in the background, watching; listening. But at least she didn't interfere when Melanie was in the company of her friends, and didn't injure anyone again. At home, Melanie endured Deedee's silent scowl at the dinner table, but she didn't have the courage to banish her.

* * *

Sometime after Melanie's tenth birthday, her mother announced that she had an appointment with a doctor. It wasn't Dr Johnson, her regular doctor. This doctor was a specialist.

"Why do I need a specialist, Mom? Am I sick?"

"No, well, um… no. Not sick exactly. This is a different type of doctor. You talk to her. I thought you might need someone to talk to."

"About what?"

"Whatever you want. Isn't there anything you want to talk about? Your father, maybe?"

Melanie shrugged. "I don't know. I hardly even remember him."

"What about the person I sometimes hear you talking to?"

Melanie glanced around furtively. "What? No, I don't talk to anyone. I just like to read books out loud."

"This is what I'm talking about. Maybe you can tell Doctor Calloway about that."

Melanie stared at the floor. "I don't know… I-I might not like that."

"Well, it can't hurt to meet the doctor, can it?"

"I guess not."

* * *

Doctor Calloway didn't look much like a doctor. She was a lot younger than Melanie expected, and very pretty, like the women at the beauty salon.

"You can call me Katie," the doctor said. "Don't think of me as a doctor, but just as a friend you can talk to."

They talked about interests like music, TV shows, favorite classes at school. Melanie found herself quickly at ease. Not once did the topic of Deedee come up.

Melanie came to look forward to her weekly visits with Katie. Melanie would tell her about her week at school, and Katie would ask how she felt about this or that.

One Friday afternoon, Melanie shuffled into Katie's office and slumped into the chair.

"Want to talk about it?" Katie asked.

"She can just be so mean sometimes!"

"Who?"

"Deedee!" she blurted, then clapped her hand over her mouth. She hadn't meant to tell Katie about Deedee.

"Who's Deedee? A friend of yours?"

"Y-yes. A friend."

"Not much of a friend if she's mean to you. Want to tell me about her?"

Melanie shrugged. "I don't know. She wouldn't like it if I talked about her."

"Well, she's not here, so how would she know?"

"That's the thing. She *is* here."

* * *

"We've made a breakthrough, Jessica."

"Nobody calls me that. Call me Jessie." Melanie's mother sat across from Katie, in the chair usually reserved for Melanie.

Katie smiled. "Ok, Jessie, I have a diagnosis for you. Melanie has Disassociative Identity Disorder. You might know it as Multiple Personality Disorder."

"What does that mean? She has a split personality?"

"We don't call it that anymore. Disassociative Identity Disorder, or DID, to use an acronym, is a coping mechanism. When a person experiences trauma, sometimes the brain will create an alternate personality that's better equipped to handle it. Think of it as rerouting the power in a grid when one area experiences an outage. It prevents overload and in many cases, protects the individual from a breakdown."

"I thought she just had an imaginary friend. She's had Deedee ever since she was old enough to talk."

"You ever notice changes in her personality? When she's Deedee, she will likely be more assertive, even aggressive or rude. Typically an alternate personality will take on those traits to "do the dirty work", so to speak. When she's feeling challenged or threatened, Deedee will come out and take over."

"Wait – wait." Jessie held up her hand. "When did we start talking about her actually *being* Deedee? Nope. No, that isn't what's been happening at all. I've never seen Deedee or talked to her, and Mel has never, ever claimed to be her. She's always talked about Deedee as if she's a separate person, even to the point of pretending she's in the room. And she hasn't mentioned her in years."

"She may not have mentioned her, but Deedee is still very much with her. She told me so yesterday. With your permission, I'd like to hypnotize Melanie and see if I can talk to Deedee."

"I don't know… it feels like we're on the wrong track here. But, you're the professional. If you really think it will help, I suppose it will be okay."

* * *

"Melanie, I want you to relax and listen to my voice. Take a deep breath and exhale slowly. Imagine you're in an elevator. You start

on the top floor and you're going to the basement. With each breath, the elevator goes down another floor.
One.
Down…
Two.
Down… Down…
Three.
Down… Down…
Down…"

Melanie had never been hypnotized before, but it sounded cool and she wanted to try it, even though her mother wasn't too keen on the idea. Katie said it would let her talk to Deedee, who had been obstinately silent ever since Melanie had told her she wasn't welcome at school. In spite of her silence, Deedee made a point of making her presence known with small acts of destruction undetectable to anyone but Melanie. She wrote obscenities and drew lewd pictures in Melanie's schoolbooks. She stuck bubble gum in her hair, tied her shoelaces in knots, and scores of other small annoyances. If Katie could make Deedee stop, it was worth trying.

"When the elevator reaches the basement, the doors will open and you will exit the elevator. You're in a nice room, with soft furniture and pretty pictures on the walls. Find a comfortable chair and sit down. Relax. Make yourself nice and cozy. Are you seated comfortably?"

"Yes," said Melanie.

"Good. Then let's begin. I would like to speak to Deedee. Is Deedee there?"

"Yeah, I'm here. Duh! You can see me sitting right in front of you."

"Hello, Deedee. I'm Katie."

"Yeah, I know."

"Deedee, can you tell me about yourself?"

"I dunno. What do you want to know?"

"How old are you?"

"You already know that. I'm ten."

"When is your birthday?"

"May 27th."

Melanie's birthday. Katie jotted in her notebook.

"How long have you and Melanie been together?"

"Forever. This is dumb. You're asking me stuff that you already know. I've told you this stuff a hundred times already."

Melanie had.

"Deedee, are you the one I've been talking to during our appointments?"

"Yeah. Sometimes."

"And sometimes it's Melanie?"

"Yeah."

"Which one of you is here the most often?"

"Me, but she thinks it's her. I let her think that."

"Did Melanie tell you not to come to school?"

"Yeah, but I go anyways. All kids should be allowed to go to school. Don't you think so?"

"Yes, of course. Do you like school?"

"Yeah. Sometimes. Except for math. I hate math. And I hate tests. And homework. She does all that boring stuff."

"Do you like Melanie's friends?"

"Most of them are my friends. She just gets to hang out with them sometimes."

* * *

Once again, Jessie sat across the desk from Katie. She didn't have high expectations for the hypnosis; she didn't believe Katie's diagnosis of DID was correct. She would have noticed if Melanie switched personalities. She knew her daughter. She would have noticed.

"Well?" she said, eyeing Katie skeptically.

"Our session went very well. I spoke at length with the personality known as Deedee, and it seems she has been present a lot more than you realize. In fact, the person you know as your daughter may be made up largely of that personality."

"I don't believe you. Deedee is nothing. She's just an imaginary friend. Nothing more."

"I asked her if Deedee was her real name, and she told me it was just a nickname. She said her full name is actually Deidre Delaina Fisher – D.D. I guess that's where the nickname came from."

"No! That's not possible!" Jessie stood, almost upsetting her chair in her haste. "This is ridiculous."

"I'd like to do some more sessions with hypnosis, if you'll–"

"No! I'm not paying you to encourage this behavior. We're done here."

"Okay, then how about if we just resume our usual–"

"No. I mean we're done. I will not be needing your services anymore. We tried it your way, now we'll do it my way." With that, she stormed out of the office.

* * *

Melanie was disappointed to hear that she would not be seeing Katie anymore.

"Why? I like Katie. She's easy to talk to."

"You don't need her anymore," Jessie said. "You're cured. Remember the hypnosis she did?"

"Yeah, kinda."

"Well, that was what cured you. You're not sick anymore. Deedee is gone and you are just you, from now on."

"But Deedee is…"

"No! Don't you even say that name anymore. She is gone, because she never existed. It was all your imagination, and now you are going to stop all of this nonsense. If I hear that name again, you will be in big trouble! Do you understand?"

"Yes, Mom."

Melanie never spoke Deedee's name again, not for many years. But Deedee was always there, lurking, leering, criticizing everything Melanie did. Most teenage girls spent a lot of time in front of a mirror, but not Melanie. She detested mirrors. When she looked in the mirror, it was Deedee who glared back at her, always with that cruel grin that made Melanie feel small and weak. She hated photos of herself for the same reason. No matter how pretty she tried to smile for the camera, the photo always turned out with Deedee's signature smirk. Deedee became increasingly bitter at being hidden and suppressed, and increasingly difficult to contain. Melanie's only recourse was to avoid mirrors and photos as much as possible. By the time she was sixteen, Deedee was seething to be released.

With graduation looming, she knew her mother would insist on having photos of her. She didn't know how she would manage to live in a house where Deedee sneered at her from the wall every day.

Eventually, Jessie agreed to a compromise – she hung Melanie's graduation photo on the wall of her bedroom instead of in the hallway where she had originally intended. Melanie avoided her mother's bedroom, but occasionally she had no choice but to enter the room and glimpse Deedee's cruel sneer. She couldn't understand how her mother could look at something so ugly every day.

* * *

College offered Melanie the opportunity to reinvent herself. She came out of her shell a bit and made new friends. She even started dating. Her boyfriend, Hunter, was forever trying to take pictures of her, but she always refused. It was the only thing they ever argued about.

One weekend at a party, Melanie had a few drinks and let her guard down. She didn't notice Hunter and others snapping pictures with their phones. Many of the group photos from the party contained her, or rather Deedee's image. Hunter and other partygoers uploaded their party photos to Facebook and Instagram, unleashing Deedee onto the Internet. With each share, a copy of each photo was made. Before long, Melanie's face was everywhere, on social media accounts of friends and strangers alike. Hunter had made sure to tag everyone in the photos, so every time she looked at social media, her face – or rather the leering face of Deedee – would pop up. Melanie was livid and broke up with Hunter immediately. If Melanie had disliked her face before, she now loathed it. The very sight of herself ignited a rage within.

She stood before the mirror in the dormitory bathroom. It was time to put a stop to this bullshit once and for all. She would conquer her fear of herself by confronting... herself. She stared at her reflection. Really stared. Gazed into the dark brown eyes of the girl in the mirror. Studied the face, so identical to hers and yet so utterly different. She supposed it was a pretty enough face. The reflection smiled. No matter how pretty she tried to make her smile look, it always looked sinister.

Except she wasn't smiling.

Was she?

She raised her fingers to her lips. The reflection did the same. She touched her lips to confirm that she was, in fact, not smiling. The image in the mirror also touched her lips; traced her fingers over that wide, leering grin.

Was she insane? Was this all a hallucination?

"Who *are* you?" she said to the reflection.

The girl in the mirror laughed, her lip upturned in a sinister sneer. Her hand, still near her face, flipped Melanie the middle finger and then spoke.

"I'm you."

"What's your name?"

"Deidre. Or Delaina. Or Melanie. Take your pick. We're all the same." The girl in the mirror laughed again. Laughed and laughed until Melanie fled from the room.

* * *

Christmas vacation came, and Melanie was home for the holidays. It was good to see her mother; she hadn't realized how much she had missed her. They baked cookies and pies together and gorged on too much delicious food. Christmas evening they cuddled on the couch watching TV, full of turkey and sipping wine. They were on their third bottle and feeling a pleasant glow.

"Mom, remember when I was little?"

"Of course. You grew up so fast."

"You remember that friend I had?"

Jessie stared into her glass, swirling the wine lazily. "Deidre, wasn't it?" Her speech slurred slightly.

Melanie sat up. "What did you say?"

Jessie shrugged. "I mean, Deedee. That was it."

"No. What did you say? Where did you get that name?"

"It doesn't matter," Jessie said. "Why are you bringing that up after all this time?"

"Because I'm worried that I might be crazy."

"Stop it. You're not crazy."

"Then what do you call it? She feels real. It's like she's still with me, inside of me."

Jessie sighed. "I was hoping this would go away in time. That you would grow up and we'd never hear about her again. But…"

"But what?"

"You remember Katie?"

"Katie, the doctor? I liked her, but you made me stop seeing her."

"Do you remember when she did the hypnosis thing?"

"Sort of."

"When you were under hypnosis, she talked to someone else. Someone named Deidre Delaina Fisher. *Deedee.*"

"Why didn't you tell me?"

"Because it was impossible. She diagnosed you with multiple personality, and I didn't believe she was right. I still don't."

"Wouldn't I know if I had other personalities?"

"Most likely, yes. I've read up on it and that's not you."

"Then what's wrong with me?"

"I don't know about wrong, but I have a theory." Jessie stood and left the room, and then returned carrying a photo album Melanie had never seen before.

"What's this?"

Her mother sat beside her. "When I was pregnant with you, it wasn't just you. I was expecting twins. The ultrasound showed two girls." Jessie opened the album and showed Melanie a black and white ultrasound image. "See? There you are. I don't know which one was you, but there's definitely two here. Your father was so excited. He was different then. He bought two cribs for the nursery, and painted the walls pink. We stocked up on twice as much little girl stuff. Two of every pretty little dress, two of every toy. We even chose names. I wonder if you can guess what those names were."

"Deidre and Delaina?"

"Yes."

"What happened?"

"Somewhere between the fifth and sixth months, two became one. This ultrasound here," she pointed at the image in the album, "is the last one we had with both of you in it. When I went for a scan a month later, there was only one."

"How does a whole baby just vanish?"

"It's not uncommon at all. My doctor said it was quite normal for one twin to cannibalize the other. Usually the stronger will absorb the weaker one. It's an evolutionary thing that keeps a species strong. I guess you were the stronger one."

"Which one am I? Deidre or Delaina?"

"Neither. Or both. It doesn't matter, because you're Melanie. I decided not to use either of the names we had chosen because it felt like killing the other one. So we chose a completely different name for you."

"Then who is Deedee?" Melanie reached for the wine bottle and refilled their glasses. Things had gone from surreal to outright bizarre.

"I think you know the answer to that. It appears your twin, or at least some part of her, has managed to live on inside of you. It's impossible, I know, but I can't think of any other explanation. It doesn't seem plausible that you would have multiple personality and that personality just happens to have the same names I chose for my twins, names that you were never told, from a twin you never knew about."

"What do we do about it?"

"Maybe we should call Katie, or someone like her. She was able to talk to Deedee before. Maybe we can reach her again. Maybe she just wants to communicate."

* * *

As it turned out, Katie still had a practice in town, albeit in a bigger and better office. She accepted Jessie's awkward apology and agreed to meet with them.

"Wow, has it been that long already? It's so good to see you again, Melanie! Look at you, all grown up!" Katie smiled and clasped Melanie's hand in hers. Jessie stared at the floor, cheeks flushed. "Jessie." Katie placed her hand on Jessie's shoulder. "I'm so glad you could come." She motioned for them to sit in a pair of comfortable chairs and took her position behind the desk. "Can you tell me what's been happening?"

"Maybe it's best if Mel tells you what she knows," Jessie said.

Melanie told Katie everything, starting with her earliest memories of Deedee. Her mother listened in stunned silence, hearing much of it for the first time. She finished with her encounter with the face in the mirror and her mother's revelation about the twin.

Katie paused in thought before speaking. "What is it you'd like me to do?"

"I was hoping you could try hypnosis again. Maybe contact this Deedee, find out who she is, what she wants," Jessie said.

"Melanie, is that what you want? You're legally an adult now, so it's your decision."

"Yes. I want to try it, and this time I want to know what she says. No more secrets. I want you to record the session."

"We can do it one of two ways. Either you can have your mother present, or we can do it in a private session, just the two of us."

Melanie looked at Jessie. "I want my mom to stay. Maybe if she'd been there the first time, things would have gone differently."

"Ok, that's fine. When would you like to start?"

"How about now?"

* * *

Melanie descended the elevator in her mind. She pressed the Door Open button when she reached the bottom. She exited the elevator into an elegant yet vaguely familiar sitting room, plush with red velvet curtains and soft looking furniture. She eased into a deep armchair.

She heard Katie's voice in the background, "Are you seated comfortably?"

"Yes." Melanie's eyelids drooped and she drifted off to sleep.

* * *

"I'd like to speak to Deedee. Are you there, Deedee?"

"Of course I'm here, dumbass. I've always been here."

Jessie jumped at the angry voice that came from her daughter's mouth. Melanie would never speak to someone that way.

Katie remained unfazed. "Hello, Deedee. Do you remember talking to me before?"

"Sure I do. And then y'all tried to shut me up." Deedee laughed. "And you thought you succeeded." She smirked. "But a lot you shitheads know. I've been here the whole time."

"I believe you," Katie said. "Can you tell me a little bit about yourself?"

"Well, you already know the story, don't you? Mommie Dearest over there," Deedee jerked her head toward Jessie, "had two buns in the oven, but something went wrong. Maybe it was those cigarettes she kept sneaking, or that little drink of wine at dinner."

Tears pooled in Jessie's eyes. "It wasn't very much! Certainly not enough to harm – "

Deedee chuckled, a dark, sinister sound. "Or maybe it was just nature," she said. "Nobody's fault, just survival of the fittest and all that dumb shit. The strong devour the weak. At any rate, one of us got devoured."

"How is it that you're still here?" Katie asked.

"Why wouldn't I be? It's my body."

"No, it's Melanie's body."

"Actually, honey, no it isn't. I'm the one who survived. I just let little Miss Priss hang around to keep me company. I could boot her anytime if I wanted to."

"How's that possible?" Jessie demanded. "I know my daughter, and I know her personality. *Melanie's* personality."

"Are you sure?" Deedee leered at Jessie. "I bet you didn't know it, but I'm one hell of a good actress. Maybe the personality you think you know is just me, pretending to be sweet little Melanie. After all, I am the strong one. She is the weak. The strong will devour the weak."

"Where is Melanie now?"

"She's asleep. And she'll stay that way until I say otherwise."

"Katie, do something! Wake her up! I want Melanie back! Melanie! Wake up!" Jessie shouted, on the verge of hysteria.

"Please, Jessie, I need you to stay calm and stay in your seat. Everything is fine. Melanie is fine. We're just having a conversation with Deedee and she deserves to be heard."

"Damn right I deserve to be heard. I'm tired of keeping quiet, always pretending to be her. Things are going to be different around here." Deedee looked at Jessie. "Do you remember when you said it was time to end this imaginary friend nonsense? Those weren't your exact words, but you get the idea."

Jessie nodded, her face flush with terror.

"Well," Deedee said, "I agree. I think it's time we put a stop to this bullshit once and for all. I'm tired of sharing with her, and I'm not waiting in that room while she gets to have all the fun." Deedee leaned toward Jessie. "I have a secret, Mom. It's been me all along. Most of the time. I let Melanie take over for stuff I didn't want to do, like chores, school work, tests, that sort of shit. But the fun stuff? That sorry bitch has no idea how to have fun. If it weren't for me she'd be socially useless. She wouldn't have any friends. And that boyfriend of hers wouldn't have even looked at her."

Jessie looked at Katie, her eyes wide. She mouthed the words, *Do something!*

"Melanie, I'm going to count down from ten," Katie said. "When I reach zero, I will snap my fingers and you will be awake."

Deedee laughed. "Do what you gotta do, Doc! I'll seeya around." When Katie began to count, her eyes closed.

* * *

"…Zero."

Snap!

Melanie's eyes opened. "What happened? Did you record it?"

"Yes, it's all on video if you want to watch." Katie walked over to the tripod and turned the camera off.

Jessie rushed over to hug her daughter. "Oh my God, I'm so glad you're back! That was so scary!"

"Is Deedee gone?" Melanie asked. "I don't feel her."

"I don't know," Katie said. "But maybe she is. I think we resolved some things today. In our next session, we can explore a bit deeper and – "

"What next session?" Jessie said. "No! No more sessions. That was too scary. I thought we were going to lose her!"

"It's not your decision, Jessie. Melanie is an adult."

"I don't know. I think I'd like to wait a while and see how I feel," Melanie said. "I will call you if I notice anything… you know, weird or whatever."

"Ok, I understand," Katie said. "I will send you a copy of the video to watch and I'd love to hear your thoughts on it. Off the record, no sessions unless you want to. Does that sound fair?"

Melanie nodded. "I will be in touch."

On the way home, Jessie said, "I'm so relieved you're ok. I don't know what I'd do if I ever lost you. Losing your sister was sad, but it's different when you lose a child you've never had a chance to know."

"Thanks, Mom. I'm just glad it's over. I think she's really gone this time."

* * *

Melanie woke, yawned and rubbed the sleep from her eyes. She looked around, confused for a moment as to where she was. She recognized the plush red sitting room from her hypnosis. She had fallen asleep in the chair, but now she was lying on the couch. The room was familiar, and on further examination she realized it was a replica of her childhood bedroom, embellished with red furnishings. There was the tea set on the little table where she and Deedee had sat for countless tea parties, set with a red silk tablecloth. Deedee had always liked red. She had begged her mother to redo her room in red velvet when she redecorated. Her mother had refused, but had compromised by giving her some red velvet cushions. Those cushions now adorned the couch where she lay and one was under her head. Slowly her memory returned, of the elevator, the hypnosis. If she was awake, why was she still in the room? She took stock of her surroundings. In place of her bedroom door was the elevator, which, it seemed, was the only exit. She went to it and pressed the button, but the button didn't light up. She pushed it again, and again, furiously in her mounting panic. How could an imaginary elevator be out of order?

"Help! Help! Let me out! Katie, where are you? Help me!" She pounded on the doors and screamed for help until she collapsed on the floor, exhausted and sobbing.

* * *

Deedee gazed out the car window and watched the landscape slip by. It was a new sensation, seeing things first-hand instead of through Melanie's drab filter. Things were going to be different now that she was in charge. Yes, very different indeed.

LUNATIC
By R James Turley

Bud jumped out of bed when he noticed the restraints he'd put himself into to sleep were torn and on the floor. He sat on the edge of the bed and put his hands over his face, trying to remember what happened last night.

If only he hadn't taken the experimental pills that promised to regrow hair. Bud didn't expect it to turn him into a hideous creature that was a cross between a werewolf and a zombie.

The first time he saw his reflection in the mirror as the creature, Bud smashed it with his fist, leaving a divot in the wall. He stopped taking the drug after that, hoping it would stop the transformation. Two months, and it was getting worse.

Two weeks ago he stormed out of the house in a rage, and needing to feed. Bud didn't know until the next morning that a male body was found with the neck snapped and bite marks on the face. The nose was completely ripped off. After that he started restraining himself to the bed. The creature seemed to be getting stronger.

His cell phone buzzed on the night stand. The screen read *Dorsey*. Chills went down his spine. Bud let it go to voice mail and turned off the phone. He'd have to come up with another excuse.

* * *

Sergeant Roger Dorsey responded to, for the second time in two weeks, a murder. Like the first victim, this one had bite marks on the face with the nose bitten off. If the poor guy didn't have identification on him, Simon Crane wouldn't have been recognizable. It took a week to ID the first victim as Dwayne Moore.

The noses on both victims were bitten off after they were dead. The killer snapped their necks. Not a pleasant way to die. Was there a good way? But having their noses ripped off, that just added insult to injury.

Detective Bud Grant finally showed up. Dorsey wondered how he'd become a cop at all; always late and never seemed to take the job seriously. Dorsey drew the short straw when he got stuck with Grant. Grant had a bit of an ego for barely working and it got on Dorsey's nerves all the time. When they did share information it was like world war three.

Roger walked up to Grant, "Why are you late?"

Grant cracked a grin, "I was with Miss Right Now and I turned my phone off."

Steam came out of Roger's ears, "Grant, on call means you're available. So don't turn your phone off." Roger turned around and stormed toward the body.

"But I'm here now!" Grant yelled.

Grant had sworn up and down that the last time would be the last time. It didn't surprise Roger that it wasn't. At thirty you should want to act like a grown up and have some responsibility. Grant must not prescribe to that thinking.

Still, Roger admired him for his arrest record, if not his cocky attitude. Grant was the one who cracked the code that led to the biggest drug bust in the city's history. He was promoted to detective one week later.

Roger was inspecting the bite marks on the body when Grant said, "What have we got?"

"We have a lunatic running around biting the noses of the victim after they kill them," Roger said, pointing to the face of the victim.

"That's either sick or crazy."

"I vote for sick." Roger blew out a puff of air, "But I wouldn't rule out crazy."

Roger and the Medical Examiner made small talk as Simon's body was being loaded into the van. They joked about Grant trying to work his way through all the women on the force as it looked as if Grant was flirting with a female officer.

"Grant," Roger waved him over with one finger. "Stay here and get details from her," he pointed to the M.E. "And I'll see you back at the station."

* * *

When Bud arrived back at the station, he sat at his desk behind Dorsey's. Roger was reading papers in a folder. Bud assumed it was this case.

Bud contemplated telling Roger about his secret. But how? If it weren't happening to Bud, he wouldn't believe it. He just stared out the window until Roger spoke.

"You gonna help me or what?"

Startled, Bud turned his head and gazed at him. The way Dorsey was looking at him, Bud knew Roger was going to ask him what he was thinking.

Bud put his hand up when Roger opened his mouth. "Let's go for a ride."

Roger seemed to be more puzzled, but didn't ask questions and followed Bud out the door.

Dorsey slammed the driver side door and barked, "Where are we going"?

Bud really didn't know what to say. Finally he said, "I need to show you something."

"What, what do you need to show me?"

Bud stared at him with determined eyes, "I can't tell you. You need to see, trust me."

They pulled up to Bud's house. His stomach wrenched at the thought of how Roger was going to react. Bud unlocked the door and led Roger through to the bedroom. Bud couldn't tell if Roger was surprised when he saw the torn restraints on the floor.

Roger shook his head, "It doesn't shock me that you're into that kinky stuff."

"That's not it," he reached for the bottle on the night stand.

Roger looked at the label, "Yeah, so?" he snidely remarked.

"I took these for a little while, and they gave me one bad side effect." Bud pointed to the restraints. "I needed those."

"What are you saying, Bud?"

"I'm the sicko that's been biting the noses off of the corpses."

Roger turned to look at him. There was almost compassion in his eyes, and Roger said, "You mean these pills turn you into a killer?"

"Not only that." Bud took out a pink pill from the bottle, "They turn me into a hideous looking creature."

Bud didn't think he believed him until Bud pointed at the mirror. Bud saw sympathy in Roger's eyes. Maybe his rough cop attitude would soften.

* * *

A week later Dorsey was working alone – Grant had been sent to a clinic in the city – when a 911 call came in. Roger got there in time to see the victim struggling for their life, clawing and scratching at the monster on top of him. Roger knew it had to be Bud.

He drew his gun and yelled stop, but Bud continued beating his pray. Bud finally looked up after Roger continued to yell. Moving closer Roger got a good look at the fangs slowly walking toward him.

"Stop right there Bud," Roger was trying to hold his gun still.

The creature kept coming. Roger steadied his gun with both hands and pulled the trigger. Bud clutched his chest and fell to the ground.

Roger quickly ran to him and rolled him over. "Bud, can you hear me?" he said, slapping his face.

Bud was dead. As he watched the monster disappear into Bud, Roger was overcome with emotion.

Star Crossed
By Juliette Kings
aka The Vampire Maman

I don't remember why Teddy wanted to go to Verona. Maybe it was the Roman ruins or the colorful buildings. It might just have been because we had never been there before. Or maybe it could have been because the vampire population is small.

I'd ask Teddy and he'd just smile and tell me that it was the romance of it all. With Teddy everything is about the romance of it all.

We'd rented a tile roofed house with a courtyard full of flowers, a hot water heater that worked, and a quick walk to the markets and historic sites.

One morning over coffee I heard someone crying. I questioned my husband. He went out to the courtyard and didn't see anyone.

"It sounded like a girl," I said. "She sounded so sad."

We both stood in the kitchen and listened. The crying started again. Then we heard the voice of a young man speaking softly in Italian.

"This is not my fault," he said. "I had no control over the situation. I told him that you were both fools to think your infatuation would lead to any good."

Then she wailed and cried again. "You are wrong. He and I were in love. It was the love that only angels can bring to this world. It was true. It was so beautiful."

"No," the young man said. "He was like a dog who sniffed at every crotch he saw. He would follow them until they shooed him away. You were nothing but a rebound with a pretty face. Nothing more than another cute little pet."

The girl screamed obscenities at him, then it stopped.

Despite it being summer, a chill filled the air. Teddy and I looked at each other.

"Ghosts," said Teddy. "I hate ghosts."

Suddenly a young man, more of a teenage boy, with hair to his shoulders and a billowing white shirt, stood before us.

"You hate ghosts, do you? I hate vampires. They come here with their breath smelling of blood, and their pale skin. Yet… look at you. Damn you are handsome. Your wife is quite lovely, but you! You, both of you, do not look, or even act like the undead demons of the night."

"We are neither undead nor demons," I said.

The wailing started again. Materializing next to him was a girl, maybe thirteen or fourteen. She wore a long green dress. Her dark hair was flowing down her back to her waist. Tears flowed down her face.

"My love Romeo and I were to be together always, even in death, but I was stuck here with HIM." She glanced over to the male ghost with hate and loathing.

"You were idiots," he said. "You had no business hooking up. I died because of you. Because of YOU, Juliet."

"Mercutio, you are a liar and a wart on the ass of a dog." Then she looked at us. "For hundreds of years he has done nothing but insult me and question my love for Romeo. He is jealous to the point of obsession."

"I would rather die than be with a girl like you," Mercutio said.

"You *are* dead!" Juliet screamed.

"Because of you. I am dead because of you. Now I am stuck with this bitch forever while my ungrateful friend Romeo has gone with the angels to a heaven he does not deserve."

"Why do you stay in this place?" I asked.

"It is where vampires come to visit. Normal living people do not see us. They do not believe in us. When Juliet cries, they only hear the wind. When we tap on the walls they think we are rats," said Mercutio. "It breaks my heart because my charms are wasted on an ungrateful child."

"I am not a child!" Juliet wailed.

"You are not a woman," said Mercutio. "So why do we stay? Where would we go?"

"My name is also Juliette," I said, "I just spell it differently."

"It looks as though you were wiser when choosing a man," said Mercutio.

Juliet started to wail again.

I glanced at my husband. "Should we go see some of the old city, Teddy?"

"Good idea," said my handsome husband.

As we walked the streets, Teddy put his arm around my shoulder and kissed me. "I'm glad that when I almost died that I woke up as a vampire and not a damn ghost. They're always so bitter."

"Bad decisions. You didn't choose to be vampire, but you also didn't choose to fall in love with the wrong person," I said.

"Very true. I'm happy to say I've never felt the urge to be star crossed."

"Or throw pebbles at my window late at night."

He laughed and kissed me again. Teddy and I have always told our children that choices they make when they are young might follow them forever. They must be careful and think of consequences. Being carried away in the moment might be deadly, or even worse.

Tragedy comes in many forms. Then again, so does comedy. I think I'll stick with comedy. Yes, don't underestimate a vampire's capacity to entertain.

Now, several years later, I sometimes wonder if the spell was broken on the two ghosts in Verona. I can only hope. Even the worst follies of youth should eventually be forgiven. It is time for them all to say goodnight. And now, it is time for me to do the same as well.

Religion Revisited
By Diana Garcia

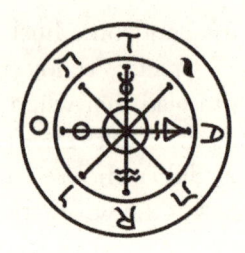

Fetid smoke in that ancient church,
Suffocates.

Diamond-dust particles rain down from stained glass windows.
Painted warring angels beat down malicious devils in disguise,
While accusing dead saints look down upon me.

The broken kneeler squeaks out in pain
As the old woman kneels to pray her rosary beside me.
Black lace veil shrouds my dead grandmother as she turns to face me.
Anguished whispers can be heard from the confessional.
I reel to feel her hand on my skin.
Is it really there?
Gentle grip that enfolds my wrist with urgency
Mouthing empty *alabanzas* and hallelujahs, and the glory be
In piercing voicelessness.
My mouth emulates hers in an "O".

Her icy touch, and presence calms my soul and I look forward,
At the shimmering and empty nave.
The wine of yesterdays can be tasted in my deep sorrow.
The blood of Christ,
It once comforted the indoctrinated obstinate child.
Cathechized, proselytized, immunized…
Beliefs and convictions died forever ago
When pain was hurled and replaced with shame.

Deviant Shadows

Remembering the unknowing Father Buenaventura
By rote instilling guilt in a guiltless guileless soul.
His dead face laughs at me in dreams now.
He didn't know.
Preaching genesis to my infertile hunger when I knelt before him
While I pounded my heart with my fist
With bowed head, and reverent intonations of,
"Bless me Father for I have sinned."
Mia Culpa
Mia Culpa
Mia Grande Culpa

The Sisters of Charity from my childhood cackle in the front pews.
Salty matrons with breathy whispers,
And with habits askew, they turn to leer at me.
I know they are long gone now.
Dusty crusts the earth they have returned.
St. Anne Seton cradles them in her ample bosom.

I feel safe here.
In the shadow of my lost innocence.
When I walked a mile upon gravel and pavement on my knees
Beneath the scorching sun.
A God's wrath.
A good little angel being told "It's for your salvation"
A payment for your indulgences.

My tiny voice sung *"De Colores"* with such exuberance!
Inculcated with persistent instruction.
And Father Kelly played the bagpipes upon the grass in the rose garden
Away from the rest of the brown sinners.
He, in the comforting shade.
Instilled with the Higher Power,
To his utter delight.
Wailing ululating Irishness howling out of his mouthpiece.
Such joy to my bleeding ears.

It all mixed with the Yaqui *Fariseos,*
And the *matachines,* and deer dancers.

Pounding staccato beats in the dust of long past Good Fridays
Where has it gone?
I am left desolate and fallow
To remember
That it all touched me once.
Goodbye grandmother.
I wear the lace veil now.
No progeny to teach the Word,
But I will breathe the frankincense and myrrh for you
No one will cry tears at my ashes.
But we will both sing Hallelujah when you grab my wrist again.

The Curious Fate of Aaron Dickerson
By Brian Callahan

Aaron Dickerson was, by anyone's standards, a simple man, with simple needs and simple desires. This was probably for the best, as it was a cruel trick of fate that had burdened him with those looks and a personality to match.

Exhausted from the labor of his life, he spent Saturday night as he usually did, alone on his front porch, drinking a Pabst Blue Ribbon. A guy he used to work with had told him there were better beers, but Aaron wasn't sure he trusted someone with such high standards so he had never pursued it.

Despite years of pickling himself with that swill, Aaron was still a lightweight and, after his second beer, fell into a doze on his porch, frightening the neighbors with his droning snore.

The moon was full and high in the sky when he snorted and woke up, staring blearily out into the street, trying to make out what had disturbed his rest.

"Is there someone out there?" the guy sitting next to him asked.

Aaron blinked unsteadily at this new voice, focusing now on this new thing. The guy was wearing a pink, double breasted suit with a white ruffled shirt. His fringe of white hair was still visible under the edge of a matching pink bowler hat. His face was round and hairless and covered with smile lines.

"Who are you?" Aaron blurted out, always at the top of his witty repartee game.

The other man laughed, "What a silly question!"

"No....really, who are you?" Aaron repeated.

"I'm the fellow who's going to make all your dreams come true, of course!"

Aaron looked at the pink clad man doubtfully, but asked, "Yeah…and how are you going to do that?"

The man in pink gestured up at the sky. "It's a full moon, so I'm going to grant you a wish."

"A wish? Are you serious?" Aaron said, looking around in case this was one of his old buddy Betz's stupid jokes. He still had to apply an ointment for the last time that happened.

"Of course, anything you wish. No pun intended."

Aaron thought about it for a moment, figured he didn't really have much to lose, and said, "Okay, I wish I was smarter."

The man in pink sighed, handed Aaron a Dictionary, and said, "Now let's get serious. What is the one thing you always wanted?"

Aaron looked at the Dictionary for a moment before setting it aside. "Uh sure. Okay, I got it. I wish people looked at me with admiration."

"Done!" said the man in pink, his eyes flashing eerily as he snapped his fingers. Aaron's sight began to dim, and then steadied, and he began to panic as he found himself unable to move.

The pink clad man looked at his handiwork, a perfect statue of Aaron, which would be delivered to the nearest museum. It would be famous, and much admired, a work inspired by the Every Man of America, donated by an unknown artist.

Aaron, trapped inside, watched with growing horror as the years went by.

Goin' Medieval
By Debra Lamb

Helen sits at her desk marking papers with a red ballpoint pen, underlining bad grammar, putting check marks next to misspelled words, writing question marks here and there, then lastly adding the grade in a big circle at the top of the first page of the essays. She looks up periodically, peering over the stacks of folders, to make sure no one is attempting to cheat off of anyone else's papers, as the students take their final history exam. Helen is an attractive woman in her forties, her black hair piled on the top of her head in a loose bun, wearing a white blouse and pleated dark blue skirt, with black rimmed reading glasses hanging from a chain, finishing off the look of a prim, albeit slightly disheveled history teacher. The timer on the desk goes off, signaling that time's up.

"Okay everyone, pencils down." A clatter of noise is heard as the students groan and set their pencils down, a few of them hastily checking off the remaining boxes on the test sheets. Helen makes her way through the aisles collecting the tests, wrestling the papers from the grasp of the last few holdouts. She sets the papers down on her desk and turns to the students. "Alright class, I'll have your exams graded, along with your essays, by Monday. Meanwhile, your assignment for the weekend is to read chapter 24. As you know, your final exam and essays on the monarchs of the 12th to 16th centuries will have a big impact on your grade, so for those of you who are not performing at your full potential, now's the time to put in the extra effort." The bell rings loudly and the students grab their belongings and rush toward the door. Helen shouts over the ruckus, "Don't forget to read chapter 24! Have a great weekend!" She watches in amusement as the teenagers try to push through the door all at once, excited to start the weekend. She chuckles to herself as she circles around her desk and sits down to grade the remaining pile of essays.

Helen plops another essay on the top of the pile closest to her. She glances out the window to see the sky streaked with hues of oranges and pinks. She's too tired to fully appreciate the beauty of it. She checks her watch, sighs to herself, and pulls herself up out of her chair. She opens the lower drawer of her desk and pulls out her purse. Eyeing the piles of essays, she lets out a grunt. "Let's see here. Ten more essays to grade, and twenty-seven final exams. Looks like I'm in for another fun filled Friday night." She places the papers in a plastic bin, along with her purse, turns off the lights, and locks up for the night. Walking to her car, she waves at the couple of stragglers heading to their cars in the teachers' parking lot. Howard, a slightly balding science teacher in his fifties, spots her from a few rows over and makes a beeline toward her. Helen sees him and rushes to her car, hoping to get her car started before he can reach her.

"Hey there, Helen!" he calls out, waving his arm.

She has her key halfway into the lock when she hears him coming up behind her.

"Shit." she says under her breath before turning around, a forced smile on her face. "Oh, hey there, Howard. What are you doing here so late?"

"I might ask you the same thing." Helen nods to the plastic bin she's holding, filled with papers.

"Ah, yes." He takes a step closer. "Well, you know what they say…"

Helen smiles and nods as they say in unison, "All work and no play makes Jane a dull girl." Helen continues, "I know, I know, but duty calls."

Howard looks her up and down. "You know, I have a fully stocked wine cellar. Why don't you take a break from being 'Miss Lawrence' and have a glass or two of Pinot Noir, accompanied by French bread and Brie by candlelight?"

Helen lets out a little laugh, "Hold on there, Romeo. First off, it's 'Ms. Lawrence', I'm more of a tequila girl myself, and I'm afraid I'm lactose intolerant." Helen sees Howard deflating before her eyes, so she quickly adds, "But I'm sure you have a lovely wine cellar. Perhaps I'll have the opportunity to see it some other time."

Howard perks up slightly, "Yes, perhaps. I'll be sure to invite you to my next gathering." He makes a gesture as if he's tipping an invisible hat, bowing slightly, and shouts out, "Happy grading!" as he heads back to his own car.

Helen rolls her eyes and lets out a sigh of relief. She puts the bin in the backseat and starts the car. As she gets closer to home, she decides to stop off at her neighborhood liquor store. She enters and waves at the elderly Asian couple sitting behind the counter. "Hey there, Lin. How's it going Sam?" They both smile and wave back.

Lin gleefully asks, "No boyfriend yet?"

Helen smiles to herself as she takes a bottle of Cazadores tequila from the shelf and grabs a can of Pringles. "Nope, not yet." She places her items on the counter. "You know me, Lin. A diehard workaholic." She pays for her items and gives the couple a playful wink.

As she takes a step toward the door she hears, "What, no scratcher?" She stops and says, "Sure, why not. It's Friday, go ahead and give me five."

Helen pours herself a shot of Cazadores and downs it. She pops open the can of Pringles and promptly chomps down on a stack of three chips, making a loud crunch.

"Hey Siri, living room light twenty." The living room light instantly dims. She starts unbuttoning her blouse as she goes to the bedroom. "Hey Siri, bedroom light fifteen." The bedroom light turns on. She continues to undress, eating an occasional Pringle as she does. She slips into a comfy pair of pajama bottoms and an old retro AC/DC cut off t-shirt.

Going back to the living room, she pours herself another shot and plunks down on her worn out couch. Her apartment is small, just a living room opening into the kitchen, a bathroom, and a bedroom. Small but cozy, and in a decent neighborhood, parking included. And with its own washer and dryer. Not bad for a single high school history teacher.

She thinks out loud, "You know, I have a fully stocked wine cellar." She laughs, downing the tequila. "Yeah, right. More like, I have a collection of box wine in my mom's basement." She cracks herself up as she stuffs her mouth with more Pringles.

She wipes her hands with a paper towel and gets herself organized. She places the remaining essays and the pile of tests on the coffee table, pulls out her trusty red pen, turns the T.V. on to an old black and white movie for company, and gets to work. The more tequila she drinks, the funnier her students' essays get. She laughs out loud as she reads, marking the papers up with the infamous red pen. After taking a break to eat the pizza she had delivered, she moves on to grade the exams.

She opens one eye, then the other, instantly squinting and bringing up her hand to shield her eyes from the sunlight streaming in through the opening in the curtains. "Ugh." She wipes the saliva from the corner of her mouth and sits up to assess the damage. Not too bad. Just the remains of a half-eaten slice of pepperoni pizza in the open pizza box laying on top of a bunch of papers strewn across the coffee table, a mostly empty bottle of tequila sitting on the floor next to the couch. She gets up to get a glass of water and grabs a bran muffin. She plops back down on the couch and sighs.

"What am I doing with my life?" She sighs again and takes a bite of her muffin. She picks up one of the essays and reads aloud. "Therefore, I conclude that King Arthur is badass and should be cloned." She laughs and a piece of half-chewed muffin flies out of her mouth. "Oh my God! These kids are morons!" She looks at the name on the first page of the essay. "Billy Fischer. It figures. You spoiled, privileged nitwit. Ugh." She stuffs the muffin into her mouth. Talking to herself with her mouth full of muffin, "Why, oh why did I have to go into teaching? Because I'm an idiot, that's why. But you get the summers off, how cool is that?!" She says this sarcastically, of course. She looks around at her apartment and tears start forming in her eyes, as she contemplates her mundane existence. "I know, I'll move and get a fresh start somewhere far away from this city. I'll volunteer to teach summer school and start saving up. Yeah, one more year at Grover Cleveland High and I'm outta here!" She stands up with conviction, then grabs her head, "Ooohh, head rush." She lays back down and covers her head with the afghan.

It's late afternoon, and Helen's saying goodbye to her mom on the phone. "Yeah, I will. Yes mom, I promise. Okay, mom…yeah, uh huh, yup I gotta go now. I love you, too. Okay, bye." She hangs up the phone and puts it down on the coffee table.

She picks up the last essay. "Lisa Yang. Okay, this should be good." She reads through the essay. "Wow, this kid really knows her history. Maybe I could get her to fill in for me for the next couple of weeks until summer break starts." She makes a few corrections and adds some notes, and then marks the front of the essay with a big A+.

She then gets to work entering the student's grades into the database on her laptop.

She finishes her task and is about to close the laptop, when she has a thought and brings up a screen with the headline, *Alysandra of Caerwent* by Helen Lawrence. She wraps the afghan around her shoulders and starts to read. She spends the next few hours reading, rewriting parts of it, taking a break to make some tea, and adding to her story. The sound of her stomach growling loudly brings attention to the fact that she's quite hungry, so she stops to order some Italian food to be delivered, then continues writing.

She's so engrossed in her story that she doesn't notice the time, and when she finally checks her cell phone, it reads 1 a.m. "Oh, wow." She looks around as if she had just returned from another world. "I guess I should pack it in for the night." She closes her laptop and goes to bed.

The next morning rolls around and Helen stretches in bed. She jumps up and starts her morning by making a pot of coffee. She tidies up the living room, places the students' essays and exams back into the plastic bin, and makes herself some breakfast. Bacon, eggs, and toast is her traditional Sunday breakfast.

As she eats, she rereads what she had written the night before, and nods her head in approval. "Not bad. Not bad at all, if I do say so myself...and I do say so myself." She chuckles to herself.

The hours pass quickly, and Helen nods off to sleep with her hands resting on the keyboard of the laptop. She abruptly wakes up and looks all around. "What? What happened?" She looks down at the laptop. "Oh, I must've been dreaming." She grabs her cell phone. It's 3 a.m. "Shit! I have to get up in three hours!" She drags herself to bed and promptly falls back to sleep.

The buzzer goes off with an ungodly sound. Helen reaches over to shut it off and forces her eyes open. She's in Monday morning hell. She showers and rushes to get dressed. She quickly drinks some coffee, fills her thermos with more coffee, and heads off to work. If she can get through the day she'll be golden, she says to herself. Just have to get through these five classes and the rest of the week, then just one more week before she can say, "Adios, amigos!" Oh, crap. Not so fast. She forgot she volunteered to teach summer school classes. And of course, she had to rush to sign up before the deadline, which was yesterday. Maybe she can back out.

But what about saving up so she can escape to a better city? To a school with better students, and better faculty members, better teaching systems. Does such a place even exist? As she ponders all of this, her first period class starts taking their seats. Helen eyes them suspiciously and takes another sip of coffee. She manages to get through her classes without climbing the stairs to the roof of the school and jumping.

One more class to go. She sits on the edge of her desk as her fifth period class chatters away amongst themselves. The bell rings and she picks up a pile of essays and walks up and down the rows of desks, handing the students their graded essays. She returns to the front of the class.

"Charlie and Stacey, please come up here." The two teenagers walk up to Helen's desk, looking puzzled. Helen hands Charlie a stack of the remaining essays, and hands Stacey a stack of exams. "Please hand these out to their owners." As they hand out the essays and tests, Helen addresses the class. "The essays I handed out myself were to the students who received B's and C's, which are the majority of you. You are the students who are going to pass this class, but who have not done anything extraordinary. The essays being passed out now are the best and the worst of the bunch. I just want you to know that for best or for worst, you can't hide among the rest of the students." The students all look at each other with varied reactions. "Stacey is handing back your exams from Friday. Naturally, since we're so close to the end of the school year, the essays and final exam are going to determine your final grade. I'm sure you noticed who Charlie handed the remaining essays to. I think we know which students are the highest achievers, and which students are the underachievers in this class. Those of you who are seniors will not have the chance to prove to yourself that you can do better, but for you juniors, you have a golden opportunity to show yourself, your family, and the world, that you have it in you to not just get by, but to excel."

Helen looks around at the faces of her students. Most of them look bored, a few are snickering, a few look smug, and one looks especially angry. Their reactions are not lost on Helen. "Listen, I'm not trying to bust your…uh, chops. I'm just trying to impress upon you the importance of applying yourself. Your performance here in this class is a reflection of the hard work that you're willing to put in in real life… or not."

Helen suddenly feels extremely self-conscious, clears her throat, and smiles nervously. She walks around her desk and takes a seat, shuffling through some papers. Without looking up, she instructs, "Okay everyone, open your books to chapter 24, 'Who were the Knights Templar'." Lisa, please read aloud, starting on page 368." The students groan in unison as Lisa cheerfully stands and starts to read aloud from the book.

Helen turns off the lights and closes the door. She locks the door and turns to leave and is startled by a tall man in his early fifties, with red wavy hair and a full red beard.

"Oh, Principal Kirkpatrick. I didn't hear you coming."

"Ah, it's my new Nike Air Zooms!", he chirps as he lifts his foot to show off his new shoes. "Do you like them?"

"Oh yes, they're very stylish. And stealthy too," she quips.

Principal Kirkpatrick's excited smile fades. "Helen, you're a good teacher. A fine teacher. I mean, you are truly one of the good ones. And you're not even that old yet. I mean, you still have plenty of good years left in you. I'd hate to see you become one of those jaded, angry teachers that start preaching to their students about how lazy they all are, or how this generation are all a bunch of slackers, morons, disappointments to their parents, a scourge on society…that if they don't care enough about the Renaissance and the Middle Ages to write innovative, creative papers that inspire, they will regret ever being born, and will surely fail in life." He tilts his head, patiently waiting for a response.

Helen stares blankly at him for a few long beats, then suddenly bursts out laughing.

Principal Kirkpatrick's serious demeanor drops, and he laughs as he playfully slaps her on the back.

"Oh my God, you really had me going that time!" Helen laughs and punches him in the arm.

He points at her and laughs some more. "Gotcha!" He looks at her for a moment, smiling. "In all seriousness, Helen, you really have to lighten up. It's the end of the school year, and all these kids want to do is to get the hell out of here in one piece. They really don't need to be lectured at this point in the game, and I don't need to get calls from their parents complaining about any of my teachers." He puts his hand on her shoulder.

Helen nods and lowers her head. "Yeah, yeah, I got it."

"Okay champ, see you in the morning." He gives her shoulder a couple of reassuring pats and walks away. She watches him as he walks down the hall, a boyish spring in his step. He seems as though he might break into a little dance at any given moment, obviously happy with his new shoes.

"Boy, he's cute. Oh, hell no, that's all I need. One more year in this hell hole and I'm outta here." Helen sighs wistfully, shakes her head, and heads to her car.

It's nighttime and Helen is sitting on the couch staring down at her laptop, her hands hovering over the keyboard as she waits for the next sentence to materialize in her head. She reaches for the mug on the coffee table without taking her eyes off of the screen and takes a sip of tea. A stroke of inspiration hits and she gets busy typing. She silently mouths the words as she types, squinching her face periodically when she momentarily stalls. She's been working on this story off and on since last year and is determined to have it finished by the end of the summer. She stops typing.

"Oh, crap," she says to herself out loud. "Damn, I keep forgetting I signed up to teach summer school. Well, there goes any hope of me finishing this book anytime soon." She lays her head back on the couch, feeling defeated. Her breathing becomes heavy as she drifts off to sleep.

Her eyes flutter and slowly open. She feels an intense chill and reaches for the afghan, but it's not in its usual place. She rubs her arms to warm herself and moves to get up from the couch, except she's not on the couch, but on the cold ground.

She stands as her eyes adjust to the blackness of the night, and the realization that she's no longer in her apartment, but somewhere out in the middle of the woods, sets in. She lets out an involuntary shriek, and quickly covers her mouth with both hands. Her eyes look up toward the sky, and she can make out the stars, which flicker brightly through the thick canopy of the treetops. Her eyes dart all around, but the only thing she can make out are the trees that seem to envelop her.

She takes several deep breaths, then shouts, "What the holy hell?!" She slowly circles around trying to get her bearings as she vigorously rubs her arms. "Oh my God, if I don't find shelter soon, I'm going to freeze to death!"

She looks around again and picks a direction by pointing. "Okay, this way!" As she marches ahead with determination, she finds herself warming up a little. She looks up at the stars periodically to marvel at their beauty. "Boy, you sure don't get stars like this in the city."

She keeps trudging forward through the thick forest for what seems an eternity until the trees start thinning out and she gets to an area where it opens up into a vast meadow. She's exhausted but keeps going until she finds herself at the edge of a cliff. She carefully approaches the edge and peers over to see ocean waves crashing against the rocks below.

A deep voice with an Irish sounding brogue breaks the silence. "Mind yourself, lest the wind pushes you over the edge."

Startled, Helen swings around to see the hulking figure of a man with wild red hair blowing in the wind. Helen freezes where she stands, not knowing what to do. With the cliff directly behind her and the man within arm's reach in front of her, there's nowhere to run. Besides, she's so completely exhausted that she wouldn't get very far without collapsing anyway.

The man holds out a strong hand. "Here lass, take my hand and come away from there."

In a daze, Helen tentatively takes his hand, and he leads her away from the cliff. The moonlight streams down on the man, and Helen is taken aback by his appearance. From his wild red hair and full beard, his strange clothes, his fur covered boots, and the sword hanging from his side, everything about this man is straight from the cover of a romance novel. They approach a black horse that had been waiting nearby in the tall grass of the meadow. Helen is in awe of the impressively large creature and reaches up to stroke its shiny long black mane.

"What a magnificent creature!" she exclaims.

"Aye, that she is, lassie," he says, patting his horse's neck. He slips his boot into the stirrup, hefts himself up onto the horse, then reaches down offering his hand to Helen. He swings her up behind him and she wraps her arms around his torso as the horse breaks into a gentle gallop, disappearing into the night.

Something slowly comes to life, sticking a leg out from under the sheet, then an arm, followed by a raven haired head. Helen peers around the sundrenched room, blinking her eyes. Nope, nothing seems to be out of place.

Helen sits up, looking perplexed, with an audible, "Huh." She gets the coffee brewing and goes to the bathroom. She turns on the shower and adjusts the temperature. She lifts her t-shirt up over her head and takes a quick look at herself in the mirror. Something catches her attention, and she moves closer to the mirror. She pulls at something stuck in her hair. "Is that straw?" She quickly turns off the shower and goes back to the mirror to examine the straw sticking out of her hair. She bends over to pick up some of the pieces that have fallen onto the floor, and as she looks down, she sees that her feet have remnants of dried mud on them. She bolts straight up.

"No, it can't be! It's impossible!" She runs out of the bathroom and into the kitchen. "I need coffee…yeah, that's it, I'm still dreaming." She slaps herself in the face. "Ow!" She grabs a cup from the cupboard and pours herself some coffee. "Okay, get ahold of yourself. It was just a dream…a horse, hay, a big, huge medieval looking guy. No, no, no, no…if that were more than a dream, there would be mud on my shoes."

She runs to the living room in search of her shoes. She finds them under the couch. Her eyes grow wide as she stares at the mud and grass encrusted in the bottom of her shoes. She tosses the afghan and the pillows on the couch around and finds the black stretchy pants she had on the night before. The bottoms of the pants have dirt and bits of straw stuck to them. She tosses the pants aside and runs to the kitchen, grabs the cup of coffee she had poured, and gulps it down. She pours herself another cup and is about to take a sip when her cell phone rings.

She picks it up. It's Principal Kirkpatrick, and it's 9 a.m. "Shit!" She answers the phone. "Hello?"

"Good morning, Ms. Lawrence. It was brought to my attention that you missed your first period class. Are you alright?"

Helen thinks fast and coughs violently. "I'm so very sorry, Principal Kirkpatrick. I'm so sick that I've been in the bathroom throwing up all morning. I didn't realize what time it was."

"I hope this isn't a case of the tequila blues."

"Nooo…I promise you, this is definitely not alcohol related."

"Well, when can we expect you back in class?"

Helen thinks a moment and then replies, "Listen, if you could please tell my second period class to read chapter 38, I'll be there before the end of the class."

"Good. We'll see you soon." Principal Kirkpatrick hangs up and Helen quickly finishes her coffee before getting dressed.

The bell rings and the students scramble to gather their belongings and head out of the classroom. Helen has her head down on her desk when she hears a tapping. She looks up to see Principal Kirkpatrick casually leaning against the doorway.

"Hey there, lady. How are you feeling? Better I hope. You sounded pretty bad on the phone this morning."

"Hey. Yeah, I'm feeling much better, thank you."

He takes a few steps into the classroom. "What do you think it was? Some kind of food poisoning perhaps?"

"I have no idea. I can honestly say that I've never experienced anything like it before." Helen stands up, collects her purse from the bottom drawer, and takes her jacket from the back of her chair. Helen locks up the classroom and turns to him, "Well, I'm off."

"I'm actually heading out myself. Do you mind if I walk with you to the parking lot?"

Helen looks at him and smiles. "No, I don't mind at all." They walk through the halls and out to the teachers' parking lot. They reach the principal's reserved parking space, but he continues walking with Helen until they reach her car. She goes around to the driver's side and searches her purse for her keys. She fishes around in her purse but can't seem to find them. "Crap. I must've left my keys in the classroom." She sighs. "I don't have the energy for this today."

Principal Kirkpatrick smiles and produces a set of keys from his coat pocket. "You mean these keys? Ta da!" he says with a flourish of the hand.

"What?! Wow, magic huh? You've been holding out on me," she says, laughing.

She snatches the keys out of his hand, but before she can unlock the car he says, "It's been a great year, huh?"

Helen stops and looks at him. "Yeah, it has been a great year."

"Only a couple more weeks to go. Well, actually just a week and a half to go."

She winks at him, "Yup. We're almost there, alright." They just stand there looking at each other for a long moment. Helen takes a step toward the car and he takes a step closer as well.

"Helen, please tell me if I'm way out of line here, but I'd really like to spend some time with you to get to know you better. Besides just in meetings, that is. Outside of school functions."

Helen gulps. She told herself she wasn't going to get involved with anyone who could possibly keep her from sticking to her plan of getting as far away from here as possible after one more year. Just one more year in this hellhole of a school and she'll have enough saved to get the hell out of here. She's going to find a place to go to write her novel in solitude. But look at that face. That rugged, boyish-manly face, and that wavy red hair and beard. As the principal of a high school, he naturally needs to adhere to a conservative look, but she can just imagine his hair blowing wildly in the wind, his beard a little longer with a couple of braids in it.

She's lost deep in thought when she hears, "Helen. Helen, are you alright?"

Helen shakes her head and chuckles, "Oh, yes. I guess I just spaced out there for a second."

He stands there stoically, waiting for a response. "I don't know what to say, Principal Kirkpatrick. I've always thought it was frowned upon to get involved with a fellow faculty member, let alone the principal."

"That's actually not a hardened rule. It's really more of a guideline. And please, call me Drew."

Helen feels her resolve melting away.

Drew takes a few steps away from the car, then turns back. "I have tickets for the Pavel Haas Quartet this Saturday night. I would love it if you would accompany me. There's no one else that I'd like to go with me, so you can take a few days to think about it. Just let me know by Friday, okay?"

He turns to leave, and Helen mouths the words, "Oh my God!" as she watches him walk away. She can't image how long he must've been holding onto those tickets. The Pavel Haas Quartet is one of the most renowned quartets in the world, and she can't believe that they're actually coming to play in her city. She fantasizes about what she would wear to something like that the whole drive home.

The next few hours swiftly pass by, and Helen finds herself curled up on the couch with her laptop again. As she types, she periodically reaches into the bowl of popcorn sitting next to her, tossing fluffy kernels into her mouth. She stops writing for a few minutes to admire the colorful sunset out the window, then changes gears and decides to do a little research.

She looks up the meaning of the name Drew. "This is interesting. Drew means wise and is possibly akin to Old Saxon…ghost or phantom… hmmm." She trails off as she continues reading. "Ugh, what am I doing? No distractions, remember? This is all I need. But it's the Pavel Haas Quartet! In my town! And a really cute, not too old of a guy has tickets! Plus, he's really funny and sweet."

She throws herself down on the couch, covers her head with a pillow, and lets out a frustrated scream. She sits back up and stuffs her mouth with a handful of popcorn. She jumps up, and talking to herself with her mouth full, says, "I have until Friday to give him an answer. I'm going to have to turn him down of course, or maybe not. Damn it, I deserve a night out. I haven't been out on a date for years. I have two expensive gowns in the closet that still have the tags on them!" She runs to the bathroom and looks in the mirror. "Oh my God, I'm getting so old!" She examines the fine lines around her eyes and pokes at the small bags under her eyes with her finger. She swipes at the tears that start to fall down her cheeks and points at her reflection. "Okay, you stop this right now. Right now! Stop being such a crybaby. Remember, one more year and you're outta here!" She marches into the living room, plops back down on the couch, grabs the laptop, and with renewed determination, starts writing again.

She opens her eyes but can't make anything out in the dark. Her hands feel the soft texture of the blanket that's wrapped around her. She snuggles her face against it, happy that she didn't fall asleep hunched over her laptop again. She's just about to drift back to sleep when an unfamiliar sound causes her ears to perk up. It's the sound of a man softly snoring next to her.

Terrified, she freezes, her eyes darting all around, trying to make out her surroundings in the dark. After a few excruciatingly long minutes of listening for any movement from the unknown heavy breather, she very slowly tries inching her body in the other direction. She feels with her foot what she guesses is the edge of the bed. Yes, it's definitely the side of the bed, so now to slither stealthily off the side and onto the floor, and on to somewhere far away from this strange man.

She manages to slide off the bed and starts crawling away when a deep voice groggily calls out, "Helena? Is that you? Come back to bed. It's too cold."

Not knowing what to do, Helen tries to crawl away faster, but gets tangled in the material of the long garment she's wearing. She can hear the bedding being thrown aside and the sound of a foot stepping onto the wooden floor causing it to creak, followed by the other foot. She hears the thumping of heavy footsteps coming toward her, and then feels a pair of strong hands lifting her up off the floor and gently placing her back onto the bed.

"You must have been walking in your sleep again, my love. Or rather crawling in your sleep."

Helen's eyes are adjusting to the dark and can make out the outline of a large, bearded man. He covers her with blankets and furs, then walks over to the big stone fireplace on the far side of the room to stoke the dying embers. He kneels before the fireplace, adding a few twigs, then larger pieces of wood, until the room is filled with the warmth and orange glow of a hearty fire. He stands and turns to walk back over to the bed. With the fire behind him, the man's face remains in the shadows. He walks around to the side of the bed farthest from the fire and climbs into the bedcovers. He turns to face Helen, the glow of the fire reflecting in his brown eyes. She instantly recognizes him. It's the same man that led her away from the edge of the cliff. She stares at him, marveling at the uncanny resemblance he has to Principal Kirkpatrick.

"It can't be. It's impossible," she says in a hushed tone.

"What's impossible, dear heart?" His eyes look intensely into hers, and then he leans in to kiss her on the forehead. "Now, let's go back to sleep." He lies down and wraps his arm around her.

"Wait."

He lifts his head up. "What is it?"

"This may sound silly, but what's your name?"

He looks at her quizzically. "Oh, my dearest Helena, you must've hit your head falling out of bed." He feels her head for lumps.

"Yes, I hit my head. Just humor me, please."

He holds her face in his hands and looks into her eyes. "My name, my sweet fair maiden, is Sir Drew Kirkpatrick. And you are my beautiful wife, Helena Lawrence. Now lay your head down, my sweet lady. You've obviously suffered an injury and you need to sleep."

Helen lies down and watches the flames dance in the fireplace until her eyes grow too weary, and she finally slips into a deep sleep.

Helen jolts awake and lifts her head up from her desk to see a classroom full of students reading from their textbooks and taking notes. She looks down to see she's wearing a sweater and pair of slacks. Nothing strange there. She touches her face, checking to see if she's real.

"Jesus." she says under her breath. "What's wrong with me?" She looks around the classroom. The students seem unaware of anything being amiss. As if on cue, the bell rings loudly and the students make a beeline toward the door.

Lisa Yang pauses momentarily at Helen's desk. "I hope you feel better, Ms. Lawrence. Have a good weekend." Before she exits the room, she cheerfully adds, "Only one more week to go!"

Only one more week to go. Wait, what day is it? Helen retrieves her cell phone from her purse. *It's Friday! How is it Friday? Where did the rest of the week go?* Helen sits there befuddled. After a long while of going over the recent events in her head, she finally gets up to leave. It's a warm day and the sun feels especially good on her face. She spots Principal Kirkpatrick about to get into his car and quickens her pace to catch him. He sees her and smiles broadly. "Hi there, Principal Kirkpatrick." He looks disappointed. "Sorry, habit. I mean Drew."

His face lightens. "Good afternoon, Helen. Boy, you've been scarce the last few days. I was beginning to think you've been avoiding me."

"No, no, no...just been really, really busy lately." He seems relieved but doesn't say anything. "I've been thinking about your offer."

He perks up, "Oh, yeah?" She pauses as if she's still undecided, then says, "Yes, thank you. I'd love to go with you."

He lets out a sigh of relief. "Ah, that's wonderful. I'm so pleased. I'd like to take you to dinner before the concert if that's alright."

"I would love that, thank you."

"Great. Pick you up at 6pm?"

"Perfect. I'll text you my address." "Wonderful. See you then." They both smile and nod and go their separate ways for the evening.

Helen walks into her apartment and looks for any signs of not being there for a couple of days. She's completely missing any memory of Wednesday and Thursday, as well as today, until she woke up in her classroom. Her mail is where it should be. Nothing is out of place. She sits down on the couch.

"That's strange," she says to herself. She grabs the can of Pringles sitting on the coffee table and looks up brain tumors on the Internet. "Something real is happening here, but what is it?" She runs into the bedroom and throws back the covers. "Aha!" she exclaims, pointing to pieces of straw in between the sheets. On a whim, she drops to her knees and looks under the bed. She sees something under there and reaches to pull it out. It's a linen dressing gown with bits of dried mud along the bottom of it. She sits on the floor holding the gown in complete shock. The doorbell buzzes but she doesn't blink. Another buzz, followed by a very long buzz. She shakes her head and gets up to see who it is. She peeks through the peephole. It's Principal Kirkpatrick. She throws her back against the door.

"Helen? Helen, I know you're in there. Your car's out front. Plus, I can hear you in there."

"Um, hi Principal…I mean, Drew." she says in a high pitched voice. "I wasn't expecting you. Uh, what's going on?"

He waits a beat, then answers with, "We need to talk. Something very strange has been happening."

"Oh, yeah? Like what? This can't wait until tomorrow night?"

Drew places his hand on the door and says quietly, "Please, Helen. This is important. Let me in."

Helen takes a deep breath and opens the door. Helen has Drew take a seat on the couch while she brings out a bottle of wine and pours them each a glass. They sit there without saying anything for a good long minute.

Drew breaks the silence with, "Do you believe in reincarnation, or parallel universes?"

Helen takes a sip of wine. "Yes, I do. But why do you ask?"

Drew reaches into his pocket and pulls out a blue ribbon with beads stitched onto it. "This is yours. But not 'you' yours. It's Helena's, which is you." He laughs, "I know this sounds crazy. But here, there's more." He reaches back into his pocket and places a silver fibula brooch in her hands. She examines the ribbon and brooch with amazement. She takes a big swig of her wine. "Wait here." She runs out of the room and returns with the linen dressing gown. She throws the gown into his arms. "There! What do you think of that?!" She sprinkles a handful of straw over his head and stands triumphantly with her hands on her hips.

They look at each other and burst out laughing. Helen pours more wine, and they clink their glasses together, saying in unison, "To your health!"

Drew sets his glass down, looks deep into Helen's eyes and says, "Marry me, Helen. I've been in love with you from the moment I first laid eyes on you three years ago."

Helen looks down at her glass, then shyly replies, "I guess I'll be sticking around for a while longer." She looks back up at him and whispers, "You can't fight destiny. My answer is yes, and please, call me Helena." They embrace and kiss.

* * *

Helen sits alone at a table with a few stacks of books on it, a big poster gracing her picture propped up behind her. A red velvet rope separates her from a long line forming down the main aisle of the large bookstore. The store buzzes with excitement as Drew maneuvers through the crowd, being careful not to spill the cups of coffee he carries in both hands.

"Whew. Made it." he says, handing Helen a coffee.

"Oh, thank God. I needed this so badly. Thank you, my darling." He winks at her.

A tall thin woman rushes up to them and leans over to Helen. "Okay, it's time. You're on." She turns to address the crowd. "Alright everyone, the moment you've been waiting for is here! We're very honored to have an award winning author, who has become nothing short of a media sensation, here with us today for the signing of her novel, which as you all know, has been on the New York Times Top Ten Bestsellers list for its thirty-sixth week in a row! So, without further ado, I present to you Helena Lawrence-Kirkpatrick, the author of *Goin' Medieval!*"

The crowd erupts into applause and cheers enthusiastically as Helen stands and waves. She shares a knowing look with Drew, then sits to greet her eager fans.

8 Seconds
By Mike Cooley

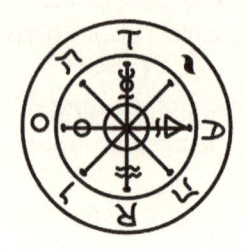

She was a waif: pink hair, pretty, full lips, sparkling eyes, painted into her outfit. But that's not what attracted my attention. Waifs were a dime a dozen. No. What made me sit up and take notice was the fact that when the bartender placed a shot of whiskey on her table, the whisky in the glass rippled, and then the glass slid across the table into her outstretched fingers. Her nails were glossy black.

I slid my stool away from the dark glass bar trimmed in chrome, and stood up. Then I walked over to her table, where she was sitting alone. I put my hand on the back of a wooden chair across from her. "Do you mind?"

She looked up, and her eyes raked my face. There was no alarm, which was alarming. "Sit."

I pulled the chair out and then lowered myself into it, feeling an ache in my bones. "Thanks."

"What the hell happened to you?" Her voice was no more than a whisper, but melodious nonetheless. She smelled like sandalwood and mysteries.

"Bomb blast. They didn't put me back together all that well." I held up my scarred hands, revealing three missing fingertips. Most of the other cracks running across my skin were hidden by my clothes. My hair was sandy blonde and my eyes were dirty jade. I was stout and a touch beyond six feet tall.

She looked around the room, maintaining an air of indifference, then raised two fingers toward the bartender, who nodded in her direction. "Mind if I buy you a drink?"

I shook my head and placed my hands on the table in front of me. Then I raised my chin and met her hazel eyes with mine. "Telekinesis." It wasn't a question.

She smiled. "Sela. Nice to meet you."

"Trap." I grinned in a lopsided way, revealing that I still, miraculously, had most of my teeth.

"It's a little early for you to announce that." Sela laughed and gestured wide with her hands. "Most guys wait until the second date."

"Never heard that one before." I raised an eyebrow. "Are you a Precog, too?"

She shook her head.

But then that's what a Precog would do. I wagged a finger at her.

The bartender showed up with two more shots of whiskey and placed one down in front of each of us. He gave me the once over and then scanned Sela with the eye of a thirsty pirate.

"I got it." I pulled a twenty out of my pocket and handed it to him. "Brad, right?"

He nodded and took the bill, then looked from me to Sela and back, raising an eyebrow. Then he headed toward a loud table near the front populated by beer drinking card players. It was the evening rush and starting to get loud as the patrons consumed more than their fair share. The air smelled of chicken wings, cheap cologne and cheaper beer.

"What are you? Besides a jigsaw puzzle?" Sela leaned forward and looked at me intently. "I usually hide my abilities, but I get lazy when I'm drunk."

"I take pills to suppress my...gift."

"But why?"

"I have a few issues." I tapped my temple with a finger. "Upstairs."

Sela laughed. "Stand in line." She drank her shot and placed the empty glass back down on the table.

I drank mine. "Why would you allow a stranger to sit down with you? People usually take one look at me and slide further away."

"I'm not afraid of you, Trap." Sela slid a hand across the table and took one of mine. "And your scars make you special. Unique."

"You see that man behind me, against the far wall, wearing a NY baseball cap?" I clenched my free hand.

Sela nodded and let go of my hand.

"Don't look at him. He followed you in."

"You're sure?"

"I am."

"I can take care of myself."

"I know you can. But my therapist says it's better for me if I punch someone in the face once a day."

Sela scanned the room again, keeping her expression neutral. "I'm finding it hard to believe that you only have one therapist."

"You're not my type."

"That wasn't a pick-up line." Sela frowned and pursed her lips. "What, exactly, is your type?"

"Still alive tomorrow." I smiled. "I think we should go. See if he follows."

Sela dropped a bill on the table and stood up. She was athletic with visible tattoos that looked more pagan than satanic. "After you."

I stood up, pushed the chair back toward the table, and turned, taking a quick glance at Sela's stalker and then looking away. He was tall and thin, wearing a cap, a white button-down shirt, and blue jeans. Over the shirt he wore a black leather jacket. I assumed he was packing heat, but I wasn't sure which side it was strapped to. He was dressed the way someone would, to avoid attracting attention.

I walked to the door and pushed through it, not looking back to see if Sela was following. After ten steps I turned around. Sela was right behind me and the stranger was just coming through the door. His left hand was reaching inside the jacket.

"Sela! Get down."

Sela whirled around and crouched.

There was a loud bang.

She waved a hand and the smoking bullet went wide, lodging in a tree to her right.

I stepped to my left and lifted both hands, clenched into fists. Then I gritted my teeth and willed energy from my chest forward. The stalker disappeared in flash of light before he could fire another round.

"What? I thought you said you took pills to block your powers?" Sela stood up, her eyes wide.

"I said I'm supposed to. I ran out yesterday." I walked up to the bar entrance, beneath a sign that read *Shelley's*, then bent down and picked up a loose board that was stacked on the sidewalk. I held the board up like a baseball bat and stood to the right of the bar's entrance, silently counting to myself.

The stranger came through the doorway again and started to reach for his gun.

I swung the board quick, smashing him in the face. He dropped like a bag of potatoes, then his body shimmered and turned into a puddle of blue gel.

"What's your power? How did that even happen?" Sela's mouth dropped open.

"Let's get out of here." I took her hand and led her away from the scene. "My power is time. I can send people eight seconds into the past."

I hurried down the sidewalk, away from *Shelley's*, pulling Sela along with me. Her hand was cool and small in mine, delicate. "Do you have any idea why the aliens are after you?"

"Aliens?"

"That guy who shot at you. He wasn't human. That's why he turned to goo when I smacked him in the face. They don't usually track humans without a reason."

"I did…take something…a few days ago." Sela frowned. She reached into a pocket of her tight black jeans and pulled out a silver dodecahedron. Then she held it up. "It's just a bauble. Why would anyone want it back?"

"So you're telekinetic *and* a thief?" I took the die and rotated it around, examining it closely.

"Well. I. When a girl can reach things with her mind, the temptation—" Sela blushed. She held her hands out, palms up.

"Don't worry. I'm not gonna turn you in. I know what this is." I handed her the silver die. "We need to go to the cemetery." I took a right down a darkened street and pulled her along with me.

Sela pocketed the die. "Cemetery? Right now? What is it?"

"It could be the reason they tried to kill you. A rare device. A ghost amplifier."

"A what? There's no such thing as ghosts."

"There is when you amplify them."

"How far is this graveyard?" Sela looked behind us for signs of pursuit.

It was nearly ten and the darkness was obviated by the shine of the moon peeking through a thin layer of clouds. The air was still hot, befitting the middle of July in New Mexico. The streets were mostly empty, with a few drunks heading from bar to bar. The smell of tortillas and green Chile drifted through the night air along with the murmur of conversations.

"It's only a few blocks. I'm beginning to think fate brought us together." I glanced over at her.

"Fate isn't real. Everything is now. There's no punishment, just a pile of happenstance that may or may not work in your favor." Sela brushed her pink hair back and squinted, looking down the street in the direction we were headed. Her jade blouse accentuated her form.

"Ah, so you're a philosopher, too." I pointed at the sign ahead. "There it is."

"Why are you bringing me here? Shot at. And now a cemetery walk. Not much of a first date."

"Let's not get ahead of ourselves, babe. I'm not your date. I'm just a guy."

"A guy who controls time."

"That's overstating my abilities."

"You're too humble. I don't date humble guys. They end up being trouble."

"All guys are trouble." I walked underneath the *Silver City Cemetery* sign, and headed toward the far end. The sadness of memory worked its way up from my heart to my throat.

I stopped near the back fence, which was wrought iron, painted black. In front of me was a granite headstone that read Mali Sundown. There were no dates on it. I knelt down on her grave. "Can I have it?"

Sela dug in her pocket and pulled out the die, then handed it to me. "Who was she? Your wife?"

"Sister. She was killed in the accident that gave me my power."

Sela rested a hand on my shoulder. "I'm sorry. That must have been terrible."

I looked up at Sela, nodded, and then placed the silver die on Mali's grave. It lit up with an eerie amber glow and began to pulse like a heartbeat.

"Mali? I need you. This is Trap."

At first, there was nothing but a light breeze in the darkness and the sound of whispers, like the rustling of leaves. But then a shape emerged from the ground, dressed as she had been on the day of the accident. She was translucent and shiny, like a ghost wrapped in plastic.

"Where?" Mali asked, turning her head from side to side.

"I'm sorry about what happened. It was three years ago, Mali. Do you remember anything?" I tried to contain my emotions. Seeing her again was like a knife to the heart.

"I remember the lab. South of Silver City. In the desert. Away from prying eyes." Mali's lips moved out of sync with her voice, as if there were a delay. Her dark hair framed her pale face. And her eyes were blue glass.

"When the accident happened, you were killed, the lab vanished, and I was…changed." I held up my hands, fists clenched, and looked at them. The scarring made me look like a jigsaw puzzle reassembled by a blind surgeon.

"Killed? I don't remember." Mali floated higher in the air. She spun slowly, turning all the way around.

"I need you to remember something for me, Mali. It's very important. You were standing at the console when the time bubble went wrong. What were the coordinates on the dial?"

"Numbers. Numbers." Mali touched her lips. Her eyes closed.

"You can do this, sister. And maybe it will change things." I looked over at Sela who was gazing up at Mali in amazement.

"36 68 54 91", said Mali, with a faraway look on her face. "108 83 73 34".

"You get that?" I looked at Sela.

Sela typed the numbers into her phone. "Got it. But the second set must be negative if it's anywhere near here."

I nodded. "What's it look like? Where did she send the lab? And when?"

"Shiprock. I don't know when." Sela zoomed in on the map on her phone.

"Mali? What was the time offset? Can you remember?"

She closed her eyes and floated in the air. A long moment of silence came and went. Then she opened them. "1140."

"What's 1140 days from 4/29/2017?" I asked Sela.

She tapped on her display. "Tomorrow."

"And how far to Shiprock from here?"

She tapped on her display. "Six hours, by the most direct route."

I stood up, restraining myself from trying to give Mali's apparition a hug. "Thank you, my sister. I will do what I can. I miss you. I love you."

115

Mali nodded and pressed her hands together. "Thank you, brother. Love always." Her ghostly figure drifted higher off the ground, and there was a faint smell of hyacinth.

Sela put her phone away and came close, wrapping her arms around me. "She's very beautiful."

"Was." I knelt down, picked up the ghost amplifier, and handed it to Sela.

Mali faded back into the darkness.

I knelt down and placed a hand on her gravestone, reciting a psalm to myself.

The die's amber glow faded. Sela slipped it into a pocket and turned to look back in the direction we had come from. "What's the plan, Trap?"

"We need to get to Shiprock by tomorrow." I looked at my watch. "It's two hours to midnight. Do you have a car?"

Sela nodded. "It's a beater, but it should get us there. This way." She headed across the cemetery to the gate, and then began walking east.

I followed. "Do you need to sleep, or can we go right away?"

"I'm wide awake. Something about being shot at, I guess." Sela laughed.

Three blocks later she turned toward the north and approached a rusty Ford four-door parked on the side of the street in front of a derelict warehouse. "Get in. I'll drive."

I climbed in the passenger seat and buckled in. "You know the way?"

Sela cranked the ignition, and the old Taurus choked to a start. "180 toward the north then 491, I think. We can follow the signs." She checked the dash, then pulled out into the street and gave it some gas.

Once we were well out of town, with Silver City and *Shelley's Bar* behind us, I leaned back and closed my eyes. "Got enough gas? I have money."

"Full tank. You wanna tell me about the accident, Trap?"

"Sure, Sela. It might help you understand."

"It's worth a shot."

"We were doing a time experiment. My sister is a physicist. Was, I mean. I was just there to help out. Take notes. Be a witness."

"And what was the experiment?"

"It was simple. Send an apple ahead a week. No muss. No fuss."

"Not sure time travel is meant to be called simple." Sela raised an eyebrow. Traffic was light. Oncoming headlights were few and far between. She kept her eyes on the road and flipped on the cruise control.

"Evidently, that's correct."

"So what happened? Did the apple explode?"

"Everything was set. Mali was at the controls. I was across the way, closer to the chamber the apple was in. It was sitting on a silver pedestal. There was a force barrier between us and the tachyon pulse emitter."

"So the controls were set to a week in the future?"

"Right. One week ahead, no translocation."

"So the apple would appear back on the pedestal?"

"Correct."

"Then what happened?"

"Mali activated the power. The whole lab is self-contained. The power source is a panel of nuclear batteries."

"And then it went wrong," Sela stated.

"And then it went wrong. The dials for setting the time and location started to spin, like the dials on a one-armed-bandit. I couldn't see what numbers they stopped on from where I was standing."

"Did the apple disappear?"

"I had time to glance at it before the explosion. It was still there."

"Is that when Mali died?"

I nodded. "There was a ripple in the air. Like the very shroud of reality was ripping open. Then there was a boom and I was spinning in the air. I looked down. The lab was gone. All of it. And Mali was lying in a pool of blood. My ears were ringing."

"Oh, that's terrible. I can't believe you survived."

"Me neither. I was pretty messed up. Only conscious long enough to crawl over to Mali and hold her hand while the light went out in her eyes."

Sela looked at me, but didn't interrupt.

"I lost consciousness after that. I guess the blast attracted the attention of the police and they sent an ambulance to scrape me up."

"How insane is it that we met? That I had the die with me? That you got to talk to Mali one more time?"

"Pretty insane." I reached over and took Sela's hand in mine.

We drove in silence for an hour. The digital clock on the dash said it was midnight. I found some classic rock on the radio and kept the volume down low.

"You still feeling okay? It's late. I can drive for a spell." I watched the dotted lines on the two lane road flicker past in the headlights.

"I'm good. I'm good." Sela flashed a smile. "Only four hours to go."

"What about you? When did you figure out you could move things?"

"When I was thirteen. It was an accident. I was at a ball field and someone hit a foul ball. It was coming right at my head. And then…it wasn't."

"You deflected it?"

Sela nodded. "Yes. But I didn't really realize it at the time. I thought it missed. It was instinct."

"How many people know?" I scanned the desert on the side of the road. It was dotted with yucca and old, dilapidated buildings. There were a few lights on in the distance. Overhead the stars shone like a tapestry of dreams.

"Not many. Most of the people who found out are dead."

"You killed them?"

Sela laughed. "God, no. I'm no killer."

"Accidents then?"

"In a way."

"What the hell?" I looked up and leaned forward.

Above us, there was a large glowing object in the sky. It arced down toward the car and then slammed into the road to our left, barely missing us.

"Shit!" Sela swerved. "What was that?"

I looked back. "Refrigerator."

"Someone's throwing refrigerators?"

"Here comes another one! Speed up." I raised both hands, clenched them into fists and aimed at the large, white missile heading for us. Twenty feet above us it shimmered and blinked away, heading eight seconds into its own past.

"Fuck. How many are there?" Sela pressed down on the gas and we shot forward. She began weaving back and forth across both lanes of traffic.

118

"Many. Too many." I held my fists up and willed the flaming appliances into the past one by one. Sweat dripped from my face. "I'm not sure I can get them all."

"Do every other one. I will dodge them." Sela was all over the road, alternating between gunning it and hitting the brakes.

Refrigerators were slamming into the asphalt all around us. The ones I was sending back in time were hitting behind us, as we outraced their future.

"How many times can you do that?" Sela glanced over. "You don't look so good."

"The effort varies by mass. The bigger the shit, the harder it is for me to make it go away."

"Why are refrigerators trying to kill us?"

"I'm guessing the aliens want to kill me…or you."

"So they rain down appliances on us while we're driving?"

"Well…that part's, unexpected."

"It's clearing." Sela zigzagged between three more of the burning objects, which crashed into the road all around us.

I slumped over in the seat and rested my head against the passenger-side door.

"You all right?"

"Yeah, yeah. Just let me rest for a sec." Sweat poured down my face into my eyes as I closed them.

* * *

"We're here." Sela nudged me with an elbow.

"Huh? How long have I been out?" I wiped the sleep out of my eyes and sat up.

"A few hours. Using your power that many times knocked you right out."

"Sorry. It looks like the sun is coming up."

"Yeah, soon. According to the coordinates, the lab should be around here somewhere." Sela veered off the road toward the imposing rock formation in the distance.

"I thought when you looked up the numbers, you meant Shiprock, the town."

"Nope. Shiprock, the rock."

I scanned the desert around us. "Today is the right day, but what time?"

"Unknown. Keep an eye out." She drove around the mighty hand of stone sticking straight up out of the sand like the plates of a stegosaurus, dodging scrub brush and yucca.

"I see something." I pointed to my right and squinted against the rising rays of sunlight streaming across my vision.

Sela turned the wheel hard, and headed for it.

As we approached the silver building, my eyes widened. "I don't believe it."

"Is it the lab?"

I nodded. "How the hell did our little experiment go this wrong?"

"I—"

"Don't answer that, Sela." I laughed and rested a hand on her leg. "Take us in and park close."

She smiled and looked down at my hand on her thigh. "Yes, Trap."

We skidded to a stop a few yards from the entrance. The silver two-story building was sitting on the desert like it had always been there. There were no tracks in the sand around it. Shiprock was looming behind us to the southwest.

I got out of the car and approached the metal door on the side facing us. "You coming?" I turned and looked for Sela.

"Wouldn't miss it, boyfriend." Sela turned off the ignition, got out of her car, then slammed the door. She walked over to join me.

I grabbed the door to the lab and hesitated.

"What do you expect to find in there?" Sela rested a hand on my shoulder.

"I have no idea. I hope I can stop the experiment, or find out what happened. I don't know how much time has passed inside."

I opened the door and stepped through it.

* * *

Across the room the apple was still on its pedestal. The overhead lights were flickering. And Mali was standing near the controls. She turned to look at Sela, who had just come through the door behind me. Near the apple on its stand, was me. Another me.

"You fractured the timeline," said the other Trap, pointed at me. "Somehow we got duplicated during the explosion."

"Mali! You're alive!" I reached out for her.

"This doesn't seem possible." Sela took a step past me, her eyes wide.

"Listen, Trap. The machine is winding up again. I don't think I can stop it. You need to leave. Take Mali," said the copy of me. He looked just like me—without the scars. He was rushing toward the control console.

Mali turned. "Trap? How can you be here? Twice?"

"You died the first time, Mali. I was badly injured."

"There's no time." The other me glanced at the controls. "Take her."

The hum of the machine was growing louder.

"I got her." Sela reached out with a hand and Mali slid across the floor toward her, without moving her feet.

Two men in ball caps and t-shirts burst into the room and leveled weapons at us. The first one fired at the other me, who was standing next to the controls.

"Shit." Trap clutched his shoulder and dropped to a knee. Blood trickled down his shirt.

The second man fired across the room toward Sela, she deflected the bullet with her mind and a wave of her hand.

I raised my fists and made one of the men flicker and disappear back into his past.

Sela reached out and flung the man that had shot the other me across the room. He slammed into the wall and slumped to the floor, then his body dissolved into a blue puddle. "Who are they?"

"They're aliens. From off-planet." I raised my fists toward the second one. "What do you want?"

"We cannot allow you to meddle with the timeline."

The dials on the console were spinning. Then they locked in place.

"Save Mali, Trap. I have to stay," said the other me. "If I can get control, I can stop this."

"The numbers. Read the numbers off!" I yelled at my duplicate.

"Come on, Trap. We need to leave!" Sela pointed at Mali and she shot out the doorway. Then she ran across the room toward the other Trap, who was standing at the console, blood streaming down his arm.

The duplicate Trap looked at me with wide eyes. "100 days, Trap. 33 39 31 31—"

"Come on Sela, we need to get out. You need to come with us."

Sela's blue eyes grew wide. "I have to help Trap. He's been shot."

I turned to face Sela, raised both hands, and clenched them, willing the energy within me out and forward. "I'm sorry."

Sela flicker and disappeared, then reappeared near the door we came in. I was feeling dizzy and weak, but I turned and willed my powers to send her back along her timeline once more. She flickered and vanished. I dropped to a knee. The lab spun around me and I tried not to black out.

"Trap! The numbers!"

"104 52 27 58," said the other me, and then his voice was lost in the shimmer.

There was a ripple in the air and then a blast. I skidded across the sand, clawing at it with my fingers.

And then the lab was gone.

* * *

"Where?" I sat up. The sun was rising toward zenith.

"It's gone." Sela reached down and touched my face.

"Do you remember the numbers?" Mali rested a hand on my shoulder. "We can find him."

"Are you the original Mali, or the duplicate from the split in the timeline?"

Mali touched her lips with a finger. "I feel real. I remember everything. Does it matter?"

I stood up, wrapped an arm around her, and limped across the high desert toward the car. My cheeks were damp and my heart beat loud in my ears. "I'm glad you're alive, Mali. You were dead in my world for three years."

"Thanks for not giving up, Trap. You didn't give up on me, and we won't give up on you."

"Do you remember the numbers, Trap?" Sela had her phone out. "I'm not sure what happened in there."

"I'm sorry about that, Sela. I sent you back to save you from the aliens. So you were never in the lab." I recited the numbers from memory as she typed them in.

"So we are going to save you? The other you?" Sela looked up at me and then back at her screen.

"Where?"

"Roswell."

"I can't just leave me to die, now can I?" I grinned.

"But what if it's a—" Mali began.

"Don't say it!" I opened the driver side door of the car and got in.

Mali got in the back.

"Trap," said Sela, getting into the passenger side. Then she started to laugh.

I looked over at Sela. "Are you with me, or against me?"

"I'd like it if you held me against you."

"Three years? I've been dead for three years?" Mali rubbed her temples and leaned forward, resting her hands on the back of the seat.

"Not you. The other you." I placed a hand on hers and fired up the engine.

"The real me?"

"Both of you were real. And you still are." Sela turned to look at Mali and smiled.

"Gun it." Mali's voice rose in defiance.

I hit the gas.

Evenings at 1123 Evergreen Street
By L.A. Guettler

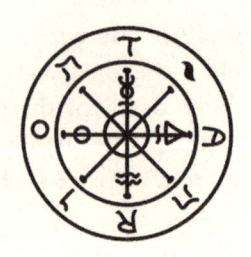

Harold and Ethel didn't drink coffee anymore, but Ethel brewed a pot anyway. She always did.

"Frank?" called Jodie. "Did you make coffee?"

"No. Why, do you smell it again?"

Ethel poured two cups and handed one to Harold. He squeezed her hand. Gently. Arthritis, you know. They settled into their chairs beside the fireplace.

Champ growled at the darkened living room. "Cut it out, you stupid dog," Jodie scolded, scratching his ears. "Nothing's there. Nothing's ever there."

The breath of sixty-three years stirred the dusty air. Jodie shivered and reached for her sweater.

"I hate this old house," she muttered.

LET'S GET HAUNTED
By Allison Ketchell

It was true, Gloria thought, that childhood places you returned to as an adult seemed smaller. But they didn't seem any less haunted. A breeze raised the hairs on her arms, but she kept her face neutral for her phone's camera. "Here it is, the Parrish House. I haven't been back here for years. No, I won't tell you how many!" She laughed and was pleased that she sounded confident. None of the dread was coming out in her voice. "If you're from northern California, you've heard of it, and you probably have an opinion about whether it's cursed, haunted, or both—or if the whole thing is a hoax. You've come along with me on a few short paranormal investigations since I launched *Gloria's Hauntings*, but this is going to be an in-depth, real-time look into the true nature of a notorious house. I tracked down the company that owns it and made an offer. I bought it sight unseen, as-is, so you're getting the first look right along with me."

She switched from selfie mode to pan the outside of the long-abandoned Victorian. It had been surrounded by a chain-link fence topped with barbed wire since she'd last been here. "It's been empty for decades, ever since the Parrish family disappeared one chilly night in January, 1959. I tried to track down remaining family members, but I had no luck. Some say they fled in the middle of the night, but others believe some part of them is still…right here."

Gloria's fourteen seasons as the host on the Real Life Channel's *Let's Get Haunted!* had helped her develop a flair for the dramatic, even if the ungrateful assholes had replaced her with a younger model, chosen for looks rather than heightened perception. She still had a loyal following, and she had been steadily building her online subscription service, billed as "Real & Unfiltered" as an NDA-skirting nod to the fakery *LGH!* had used for ratings, over her protests. Snagging the Parrish House had doubled the income from her solo project, and she hoped that was just the beginning.

Deep breath. Time to go in. "Okay, here we are. Wow, that cherub over the mirror looks pissed. I guess he doesn't like chintz." She sneezed. "These dust covers are going to have to go to the dumpster. Let's do a quick walk-through to see what condition the house is in, get some light in here, and place some sensors. I plan to sleep here tonight. Premium subscribers will get live updates if anything unexplained happens in the wee hours. Everyone else will wait until the morning report."

The large fireplace dominated the front room. Little porcelain figures decorated the dusty mantelpiece: a shepherdess, a goatherd, a girl with a basket of vegetables. The dust was thick. She'd have to tackle that later or she'd be coughing up a lung. There were no overhead lights, but she'd prepared for that, bringing several standing lamps so she'd have some light in each room. She plugged one in and crossed her fingers. "Yes! The electric company came through!" She'd been tempted to check out the house before the on-air walkthrough, to make sure she didn't have flashbacks and freak out, but she had integrity, unlike some producers she could name. When she stepped onto the third stair, it creaked, and the memory of that night came rushing back.

"Wow, the last time I was in this house, I came flying down these stairs. A group of us had broken in and set up a Ouija board in the attic. I think we contacted…something." She didn't have to fake the shiver. "At that time, I couldn't sense spirits. It was just a game. After that night, otherworldly energy was always with me, and I got used to its presence, but then—it was terrifying. When this stair creaked, I thought it had caught up with me. I didn't know what 'it' was, and I didn't look back. I sensed something back there, and I just kept moving, straight out the front door. I was the first one out. The others met me outside and we waited for Monica. And waited. And waited. Eventually, we went home before we could get in trouble. Monica was always playing pranks, so we thought, we hoped, that this was one of her jokes. Maybe she'd even rigged something in the attic to make us think the Ouija board had done something real. But she was gone. She'd been planning to run off with her older boyfriend, and we told ourselves she'd seen an opportunity that night. But we'll never really know, unless the house gives us some clue during this investigation."

The other bedrooms were unremarkable, but the nursery gave her pause. "I guess there was a baby when the Parrishes disappeared. That baby would be, what, sixty? if he or she was still..." She picked up a porcelain doll from the crib. "Probably she, I guess. If anyone has any idea of her whereabouts or identity, send me clues. I'd love to find out why they left that night. If they left."

Gloria felt colder and colder as she pulled down the ladder for the attic. "Someone must have replaced the ladder sometime since my little adventure here. Of course, the police must have looked in this house as part of the investigation into Monica's disappearance." Her feet felt heavy as she climbed up, but all of a sudden, her head was above the floor level, and there it was. "Wow, our Ouija board is still here." She scrambled the rest of the way up, pulling a lamp up behind her. When she switched it on, dust danced in the puddle of light. "Oh, the planchette is way over here. We ran out pretty quickly. One of us probably tripped on the board." She moved the board and planchette to the top of a stack of boxes. "I don't feel anything in particular here, just the low-level emanations from the whole house."

She took a deep breath and coughed. She was surprised that only the dust was bothering her up here. "Well, that was anticlimactic." She moved to the charred portion of the wall and reached toward the large crucifix hanging there. "You can see here where the fire was. There's a cupola and a widow's walk up on the roof, but the cupola burned years before the Parrishes moved in. It was said to be boys playing up there who started the fire. I couldn't find anything about the boys, so we may have another mysterious disappearance linked to the house, or it may have just been an accident. At any rate, the family living there at the time just boarded up the access point and left it with no attempt to repair, which makes me think something unpleasant happened, especially since they hung a crucifix here. Huh, I wonder if an exorcism was ever attempted. I'll have to check local church records."

"We'll look more closely up here, since at least two strange experiences are linked to this particular part of the house, but I need to get things set up so I can actually sleep in the house tonight, so we'll save that until later. I expect to spend weeks, if not months, investigating this house. I will travel to conduct some shorter investigations during that time as well, but this is my primary project for the time being. We'll dig into the history of the house, try to track down former residents, and look for evidence of hauntings, curses, or other paranormal phenomena. In a house like this, there may be several things going on."

* * *

The dust covers were in the dumpster, she'd vacuumed pounds of dust from the large rug and hardwood floor of the front room, and she'd pushed back the furniture to make room for her camp bed. Gloria sat cross-legged on the floor and opened her laptop. She liked to end the day with some interactive content. The fans really liked being able to contact her directly, and having their questions answered in real-time boosted engagement and popularity. "This is Gloria Birch, reporting live from the Parrish House in Brentcliff, California, where I once had a seance that ended with a friend disappearing. There are weird occurrences connected to this house, and we're here to investigate for as long as it takes to uncover all the mysteries. You can check out the first-look tour we did earlier today in the video section, and don't forget to tip. If you want to be first on hand if anything weird happens in the wee hours, hit the 'premium subscription' button. I'm ready to take your questions."

There were always a few creeps making suggestive comments. If they were free accounts, she blocked their access, but if they paid a subscription fee, she contented herself with taking their money and ignoring them. She read through the questions pouring in, and fielded a few about the house's history, her past experiences, and her methods. "Ah, Bobby from Humboldt, I've set up motion-sensor cameras, vibration detectors, and voice recording in each room. I'm not a fan of electromagnetic detection for paranormal investigations, though that was big on *Let's Get Haunted!*, because I expect a house like this is awash in abnormal electromagnetic energy. I want to first focus on sound and images that might show up overnight. I have an instant-read thermometer at hand to check for temperature drops. And yes, Leah from San Antonio, I have my Spidey-sense, though I don't usually call it that. And I try to back up my feelings with objective measurements and recordings. Let's call it a night. I'll let you know if anything exciting happens! Otherwise, see you in the morning."

She'd started to close her laptop when a message caught her eye: "Do you really think you'll get out of there alive?"

Trolls.

* * *

Gloria tried to sit up, but she was trapped, flailing around in the dark, heart pounding, until she remembered she was in a sleeping bag and extracted her arms. What had woken her up? She listened closely but didn't hear anything unusual. A breeze cooled her bare arms and she shivered. Wait—breeze? Why was there a breeze? She switched on the light, but nothing looked out of place. The breeze was coming from the fireplace. The flue must be open. She checked her phone: 3:20 a.m.

She flipped open her laptop and sent a push notification to the premium subscribers. "Anyone up? I was just awakened by a gust of wind coming from the direction of the fireplace. The room is chilly." She held up the instant-read thermometer. "Temperature in the room is 58 degrees. Outside temp is 61. All windows are closed. Today's high was 72 degrees. No way the house should be this cold." She watched a few insomniacs and East Coast fans express their excitement. "I'm going to check out the fireplace. I guess it's possible the flue has been open all these years, or maybe something jogged it open, but I didn't notice the house being cold before now."

Gloria wasn't really afraid of ghosts. Except for the occasional poltergeist who threw things around, they mostly just wanted to be noticed. But she still felt a creeping dread as she approached the fireplace. She jumped as a gust of wind blew around her feet, swishing the t-shirt she wore as pajamas. "Let's check the flue."

She shined the flashlight up the chimney. "I'm hoping I'll see more when I review the recording. It's mostly just dark up here." She coughed. "And dusty. The cupola that burned so many years ago is beside this chimney on the rooftop. I wonder if the spirit energy is concentrated in this—" *Clunk. Clunk.* She reached up slowly with her hand. "The flue is closed, but that doesn't mean there's not a gap letting in a draft." *Clunk.* The flue vibrated above her fingers. "Something is hitting the flue from above. I can feel it. Maybe a trapped bird?" She was concentrating too hard to feel terrified when the flue gave way under another clunk, flinging her hand against the sooty bricks of the chimney. She scrambled out just as something fell into the fireplace. It looked like a pile of dirty cloth, but sounded heavier.

"Something was up in the flue. It looks like a pile of clothes or a wadded up sheet or something. It's dirty from the chimney. It's now 68 degrees in here. Maybe whatever was trying to get my attention with the cold wind just wanted me to find this." She was strangely reluctant to approach the bundle. She touched it and her hand came away sooty. "It feels like a sheet and looks like it had a flower pattern on it. It's pretty faded. There's something hard inside, but not one large solid object, more like a bunch of little things." Bones, she thought. Monica's bones. The baby's bones. She slowly unwrapped the bundle, and little porcelain figures like the ones on the mantel fell to the floor.

"Huh," she said, trying to sound casually amused. "What are these doing up here? Whether it's human or spirit mischief remains to be seen. A ghost might cause a draft and use this to get my attention. Are the figures a clue to the weird occurrences in this house? Or did some human stuff them up there? I assume no fire has been lit since the Parrishes left, so they must have been placed there before then. Are they valuable and someone wanted to hide them?"

"*Antiques Roadshow* crossover!" someone commented. She laughed and read it aloud. "Maybe I can pay off the mortgage with these. Who knows." She lined the little figures up on the mantel, unconsciously switching them around into an order that seemed right. She stared at the apple-cheeked little girl holding a doll and wondered if she was in over her head.

"Well, I'm going to get some more sleep now that it's warmed up in here and I'll look around more when I wake up. Thanks for keeping me company, guys!"

She shut the laptop and got back in the sleeping bag. She felt uneasy and confused. What was the purpose of this? Teenagers playing pranks? One of the Parrishes keeping valuables safe? A workman stowing them to steal later? Was it a clue to the disappearances and the fire? She felt suddenly exhausted and fell into a dreamless sleep.

* * *

Gloria felt better in the morning. One of her fans had live-tweeted his excitement over the late-night ghost update, and it had gained traction while she slept. Several of the content-farm sites were running stories about her. Her subscriptions were up, and she'd pulled in quite a bit in tips from the lucky people who'd watched the livestream. The *Let's Get Haunted!* producers hadn't thought she could still bring in the viewers, and here she was, popular even without chairs flying around the room or creepy whispers piped in. Real haunting was even more dramatic than the faked stuff. You didn't need to embellish.

"Good morning, everyone, and welcome to my new members. After the excitement with the fireplace last night, nothing else happened. I slept like a baby." Baby. The baby upstairs, clutching her doll, she thought, shaking her head to erase the image. "Anyway, today in boring tasks, I have to get the rest of the dust out of the front room so I can breathe in there. I don't want to have the furniture removed because it's been here so long it's almost part of the house, but I've rented a steam cleaner to attack it, and I've got a particle mask and eye protection for dusting the surfaces. I'll spare you the live footage of that process. Before I get to that, though, let's see if any of our sensors recorded anything during last night's event."

Gloria opened the program she used to collect data from her sensors. "Nothing from the motion sensors, except of course in this room. Let's see if it picked up any motion that wasn't me tromping around. It doesn't look like it, but the vibration detector picked something up near the fireplace when the bundle dropped down onto the flue in the chimney. It didn't occur to me to put a camera or recording equipment in the chimney. If there was something to see, that's probably where it was. I can move some equipment from one of the other rooms in case that's the focal point of any other incidents. The attic equipment picked up some sound. Don't get too excited. It's often squirrels or bats or something in attics. I'll pull up the footage the motion-sensor cameras picked up and play it along with the sound."

The screen filled with the image of the dim attic. A shimmer appeared in front of the boarded-up area, and expanded and thickened into a white fog, roughly spherical in shape. Gloria had seen ghosts before, but she still gasped. Comments began to flow in, mostly in all caps and many R-rated. "This is bigger than the usual ghost form. It may not be a single spirit, but a concentration of energy. Look! It's sort of flattening against the wall." It was still silent, so she checked the sound. "It's not talking, whatever it is. It just disappeared behind the chimney wall! This is 3:20 a.m. exactly, the moment I was woken up by the gust of wind down the chimney." She went back a few frames and hit pause. Whatever this was, it was trying to get her attention. There was a whooshing sound and a couple of distant clunks that must have been the bundle falling down the chimney. She watched to the end, but the fog didn't reappear before the camera turned back off.

"What are we dealing with here? Is this what contacted us through the Ouija board years ago? If it's not a single spirit, that might explain why we didn't get a coherent message, just a rush of energy. But what is it?"

Her notifications were pinging again and subscriptions and tips rolled in. Someone major must be live-tweeting. She had a sudden thought that she should leave. Just walk away from the house, the money, ghosts in general. Get out while she still could. Was this the part in the horror movie where the audience would be yelling, "Just leave! Run away!" as the main character made stupid choice after stupid choice until something killed her in a horrible way? She shivered. Time to ground herself with some errands and dusting.

* * *

The living room was almost inhabitable when Gloria stopped to shower, eat lunch, and check messages. Nothing strange had happened during the morning, but last night's demonstration had taken serious energy. The spirits might be exhausted today. People thought that ghosts were more active at night, but really that's the only time humans weren't too busy to notice them. If you were tuned in to the ghost world, you'd see them at all times of day.

Her notifications were exploding again. Someone had posted a screenshot of the white entity on Instagram, a clear violation of her terms of service, but since it had gone viral and expanded her subscriber base yet again, she would overlook it. Just some fan mail, and…oh. "Hey, Gloria. It was weird to open Twitter and see you back in that house after all these years. Be safe, okay?" It was signed Benjamin. Her high school boyfriend. She'd lost touch with the kids she'd broken into this house with, and even if it had occurred to her to give them a heads-up about her plans, she wouldn't have known how to track them down. It was strange to think of Ben watching her from afar, but oddly comforting. She hit 'reply' but had no idea what to say. Well, it could wait.

She was distracted by Ben's message as she started the afternoon update. She could ask him what he remembered from that night, and whether he knew how to reach the others. They might have valuable insights about what they'd experienced. Sure, they'd talked about it as teenagers, but maybe their views of events had changed over the years. Why hadn't she thought of that before? She was strangely reluctant to involve them. What if she invited them all to the house? They could have another go at the Ouija board. She grimaced at the idea. Was it repellent because it was tacky and exploitative, or because it was dangerous? Maybe both.

"This morning, I dropped off the crucifix at a local antique store to see if I could get an idea of when it was put up on the attic wall. I was curious if the original owners of the house boarded up the roof access and hung it up there, or if some supernatural occurrence had prompted the Parrishes to hang it, or someone else. I don't remember if it was there when I was last in the attic, but then, we weren't looking closely at the walls, and we only had flashlights then.

"I just got a call back from Savoy's Fine Antiques"—she'd traded an on-air mention and a social media post for a free appraisal—"and Geoff Savoy tells me the crucifix definitely dates from the 1920s, so this crucifix could have been here when the Parrishes moved in, and they chose to leave it there. Why? They clearly used the attic. It's still cluttered with boxes from the 1950s. It's hard to imagine how they could have overlooked it for so many years. Were they religious? Superstitious? Or had they been warned about the house and didn't want to tempt fate?

"When I looked through the church records for an exorcism—there's no record, but the current priest tells me that one may have been performed but not recorded—I also checked and found that the Parrishes were not members of the Catholic church, so leaving up the crucifix seems strange. Okay, this afternoon we're headed back up to the attic to see how we can reopen the roof access."

The comments were a mixture of thrilled and apprehensive, with several people suggesting that she should leave it the way it was, especially since she'd taken down the crucifix. She was privately nervous, which was part of the reason she was checking it out during the day and not after dark. She was citing better lighting and visibility as her reason, and, well, that was partly true.

Back to the attic. "You know, the brick behind where the crucifix was doesn't look burned at all, but the surrounding wall is covered in soot. I wonder if it was hanging up here before the fire. Huh." She rested her hand against the brick and felt a pulsing energy. She jerked her hand back. "Something is concentrated in the chimney. Okay, now for the boarded-up roof access. Let's pry off these boards that were nailed over it." She'd brought a tool box and several power tools, but the rotten wood crumbled when she dug into it with the prying end of her hammer. "Oh, this is going to be easier than I thought." She quickly removed the boards and peered inside. "Lots of ash."

She came back with a broom and dustpan and a ladder. "Let's sweep some of this ash out so I can set up the ladder safely." As she swept, something clunked against the wall. "Another surprise, huh? This house is full of them. Let's see what we have here." She stirred the ash around with her broom and found two more porcelain figures. She wiped off the ash and saw a boy pulling up a bucket from a well and a boy fishing. "Ah, more of these. I'm getting quite a collection. I'll have to take these to the antique store too. They remind me of something my grandmother had, but there's no artist's mark or anything. Well, I'll bring them downstairs and put them with the others until I can take them in tomorrow."

Gloria climbed up the ladder and poked her head up over the roof. Very little of the wooden cupola remained, just a few charred posts. "I really don't feel anything in particular up here. Maybe this was just an accidental fire and the family closed off the roof afterward." She looked uneasily at the chimney. "That was anticlimactic, but it's like that sometimes. Now we don't have to wonder what's up here."

Once downstairs, she added the boys to the lineup of porcelain figures. "I could have sworn the goose girl was lined up with the rest, but it's off to the right now. Weird. I've spent too much time looking at these things, I guess."

Before she went to bed, she did a last chat session with her audience. She answered a few questions before stopping short. "Candace from Castle Rock, Maine, are you positive the goose girl was on the other side?" Gloria looked at the attached screenshot. Of course, it could have been photoshopped. But then more screenshots and comments came flooding in. She sat back and thought. She did keep looking at the figures whenever she passed them. Maybe she'd been moving them around without realizing it. She suggested this but one of her fans was able to show that the goose girl had been on the left when Gloria went back upstairs with the ladder and broom. When she'd returned, it was on the right.

She got up and studied the piece. It looked just like the others. Apple-cheeked girl in a bonnet, holding a goose. Gloria had been chased by nesting geese before, so she felt this was unwise on the girl's part, but there was nothing else remarkable about the figure. "I'm not sure what moving this one figure is supposed to tell me, but they'll all go to the antique dealer tomorrow. Maybe he can give us some insight about these. More information on where they came from, who made them, all that might be helpful. Well, good night. See you in the morning, if not before then."

* * *

Gloria was suddenly wide awake. She opened the laptop and checked the monitors. "Something woke me up. Let's see…it's 1:22, and the temperature is normal. No sounds, motion, or vibrations picked up by the equipment. I don't hear anything now. Wait! A knocking? It's coming from the direction of the fireplace, upstairs maybe? Let's go check it out."

She forgot to step over the creaky stair and startled herself on the way up. "I need to have that thing fixed before it gives me a heart attack," she muttered. On the landing, she listened closely. "No, it's still above me. I guess we're going into the attic." Her feet felt heavy as she trudged to the trapdoor. One foot after the other up the ladder. The white fog she'd seen in the video was even more impressive in person. She walked toward the sphere, mesmerized. It was bright enough that she didn't need to turn on a light.

She tripped over something. "The Ouija board. I moved this and something moved it back." Gloria laughed. "Well, I wanted a clearer message. I was too dense to figure out whatever the figurines mean, so it—or they—decided to make it obvious." She walked over to the fog and reached out her hand. "It's like being in cold water."

She set her phone down so it had a view of both the Ouija board and the fog. She slowly sank to the floor, touching the planchette lightly. Maybe it was her imagination, but she thought the fog swirled in approval. She'd have to check the recording later. "I feel like I should say I always knew I'd end up back here or something, but this is a surprise. I honestly don't know what will happen. Maybe nothing. But maybe I'll find the answers we're looking for." She moved the planchette to the starting point and took a deep breath.

***

"Welcome to a Very Special Episode of *Let's Get Haunted!* This is Ellie Costa, reporting live from the Parrish House in Brentcliff, California, where a former host went missing during either a publicity stunt or a tragic paranormal occurrence one year ago today. We've been trying to get access to this house ever since Gloria Birch disappeared under mysterious circumstances that she live-streamed as part of a paranormal investigation. We've all seen the footage and analyzed it frame by frame, trying to detect any doctoring or spot some trick Gloria used to make herself appear to vanish, but there's been no sighting of her in all this time, so it's pretty far-fetched to think it was a publicity stunt. Tonight, on the anniversary of her disappearance, we're going to spend the night in the house and get to the bottom of this mystery."

She entered the front room and sneezed. "We'll have to get a cleaning crew in. This is some serious dust. Look! Here are the little porcelain figurines that featured so heavily in Gloria's story. She claimed to have found some of them in the chimney, others in the attic."

Ellie touched the figures one by one, leaving little finger marks in the dust. "I think my grandmother had some of these. Shepherdess, goatherd, girl with vegetables, goose girl, girl with a doll, boy at a well, boy fishing, girl sitting in a tree. I don't remember that one from the footage. Anyway, did Gloria plant the figurines to add some spice to a boring investigation? Was the light show in the attic rigged? What went wrong the night that Gloria disappeared? Are you ready? Let's get haunted!"

Nightmare in the Nursery
By R James Turley

Tim and Christi Muldoon bought their dream home in Northbrook, twenty-five miles northwest of Chicago, not long before they were married five months earlier. Instead of a honeymoon, they settled into the house while setting up a nursery for the bundle of joy Christi was having in two months.

After they found out she was pregnant, they decided to be surprised, and not know the sex of the baby. Both of them made a list of baby names they liked, and compared them. Six of the names matched, three for girls and three for boys. They picked their two favorites, Christopher and Darla. Tim had always said he wanted a boy, but like his wife, he'd rather have a Darla running around the house.

* * *

Tim had made an arrangement with the Daily Herald to work and write his column from home so he could help with the baby. He made the den into an office space. The desk ran along the back wall facing the front window. A couch sat to the left of the entranceway, facing a TV along the side wall across the room, and a pool table in the middle of the room.

With Christi gone for the day with her mother, Tim had time to work on his novel idea. He wanted to write a mystery with a little romance thrown in. It didn't take him long to come up with an opening scene, and he jotted down the summary on an index card. Before long, the scenes flowed out of his head.

Tim had opened up his laptop to write the first scene when he heard a loud thud coming from upstairs. Maybe a bird had somehow gotten into the house and hit the wall. In the upstairs hallway, Tim didn't see anything. Nothing had fallen or seemed out of place in any of the rooms. After he had double-checked, Tim went back down to his office.

Two scenes and an hour later, Tim felt a little hungry, and made his way to the kitchen for a sandwich. He opened the fridge and collected lettuce, tomato, ham and mustard, and then kicked the door shut. Something didn't seem right. *Did the light come on?* He set the food on the counter, and opened the fridge again. Falling back in a start, he scarcely missed bumping his head on the freezer's handle. The door shut, and Tim quickly got to his knees and opened it. Whatever had made Tim jump back was gone.

Feeling better after having eaten, Tim went back to work. But he couldn't stop thinking about the fridge. *Did I see what I think I did?* The more he thought about it, Tim realized what he did see. It was a silhouette of a little girl's head.

It couldn't be. The stress of becoming a father must be getting to him. He shut the laptop, stretched out on the couch and was quickly fell asleep.

Tim looked at his watch when he awoke.

"Two hours." he sat up.

Christi must have heard him and rushed in. She leaned over the arm of the couch and kissed him.

"Why didn't you wake me when you got home?" he said, sounding annoyed, more with himself.

"I just got home a little bit ago. You look so adorable when you're sleeping." She smiled and giggled.

He stood, grabbed her hand and led her to the kitchen. Opened the fridge.

"What do you see?"

She looked at him like he was crazy, then gazed into the fridge. "Milk, eggs, ham let..."

He slammed the door shut and turned his back to her. "So I didn't see anything. Either that or I'm going crazy."

"Honey," she drew it out. "What the hell are you talking about?" She put her hand on his shoulder.

He pointed at the refrigerator door, laughed and wiped his hand over his face. "I swear," he raised his right hand. "I swear I saw a shadow of a little girl's head."

"You had to be dreaming."

He opened the door, "I didn't realize at first; the light never came on when I got the food," he pointed at the light. "I put everything on the counter, and opened it again, jumped back when I saw it."

Putting her balled fists on her hips, "That had to be one hell of a dream."

"Why don't you believe me?"

She cupped his face. "I believe that you believe it."

Unable to find the words to argue, Tim threw up his arms and went back to work. He could feel her stare as he walked down the hall.

The next morning, Tim opened his eyes and just watched her sleep. Her round belly gently rising and falling with every breath; a beautiful sight. How did he get so lucky?

Tim had almost fallen back to sleep when he felt her jerk out of bed.

"What's wrong?"

"I heard something in the baby's room." She slid into her slippers. "Like a muffled cry. Get up, come with me."

"I didn't hear anything," he said, putting on his robe, "You sure you weren't dreaming?"

She gave him an annoyed look. "Just come on!" she walked toward the door.

Tim pulled her behind him to go in the opened door first. Maybe Christi didn't hear anything, but after what he saw yesterday Tim wasn't going to take a chance if something or somebody was in there. He held up his hand in front of her, telling her to stop, took a deep breath, and went in.

"Did you take the stuffed penguin out of the crib?" he said, walking to the crib.

A look of fright came over her face as she shook her head, "It was there when we went to bed."

"Then how did it get there?" He pointed under the crib

"I don't kn..." she stopped talking and listened.

"What is it?"

"Sh," Christi held up one finger. "Did you hear that?"

A soft, continuous knock came from the wall behind the crib. A whimper, like a puppy's cry could be heard every few minutes. Tim pounded on the wall. The knocking stopped but the whimpering got louder. After a few minutes, it also stopped. Tim picked up the toy, set it in the crib and led Christi to their room.

Later in the afternoon, a pounding on the front door interrupted Tim from writing his weekly column. Before he answered the door, he checked in the living room to hear Christi snoring on the sofa. Watching soap operas would put anyone into deep sleep.

No one was at the door.

Before going to bed, they looked into the nursery. On the tree painted on the wall behind the crib was a little girl hanging from a branch with a noose around her neck. Christie screamed, and ran into their bedroom. Tim quickly followed her.

"Call the cops," she looked up at him with tears in her eyes.

Tim sat beside her on the bed. "There has to be an explanation."

"Yeah, this place is haunted," her voice rose.

"Don't get excited."

Christi let out a puff of air, "Just call the damn cops."

Tim did what she asked, although he thought it was a waste of time. How the hell was he supposed to explain it over the phone? Twenty minutes later, Officer Bird was at the door. The officer followed Tim upstairs to where Christi was waiting. All three of them went into the nursery to look at the wall, but the hanging girl was gone. Tim was dumbfounded, and after some questions, Officer Bird left.

What was going on? A painting on the wall didn't just appear and disappear. There wasn't any point in arguing about it that night. Their bed was calling, and they'd deal with it in the morning. But how did one sleep after seeing what, or wasn't there?

* * *

Christi was startled awake. She sat up in bed in a cold sweat and her heart pounding. It was still dark, so she decided to let Tim sleep. She needed to process what she'd seen in her nightmare: a child crying as it was being buried. Christie hadn't had that dream since she was twelve. It seemed so real this time.

She waddled her way to the kitchen for some warm milk to calm her nerves. She would have preferred a stiff drink, but not while she had a bun in the oven. Could there be a connection between her dream and the strange things going on in the house? She had to find out.

After lunch, Christi started researching online about the house, hoping to learn who the previous owners were. Luck was on her side. Joe and Donna Dunlap had owned it a year before she and Tim moved in. The realtor did say it had sat vacant for a while. Joe and Donna had a daughter, Abby. It didn't say what had happened to them.

The computer screen went black, and the keys started typing by themselves. Wanting to jump out of her seat, she couldn't. Christie tried to scream, but nothing came out. The words "help me" appeared on the screen.

She managed a faint yell while slapping her hand on the dining room table. Tim rushed in, and she wrapped her arms around his waist and sobbed.

"What's wrong?" he rubbed the back of her head.

Pointing at the computer screen, Christie whispered, "It typed by itself."

"The computer typed itself? What did it type?"

She looked up at him and wiped her cheeks. "Help me."

She nodded her head when he asked if she wanted something cold to drink, and he went into the kitchen. The refrigerator door slammed. Christie ran into the kitchen to see Tim white as a ghost, and his eyes ready to pop out of his head.

"What did you see?" she opened the fridge but saw nothing.

"Light, eyes, red," he babbled.

"Breathe," she put her hands out in front of her and pushed down. "In, out. That's it."

He took a breath, "The light flickered, and I saw these eyes. They were red."

A scream came from upstairs. It jarred Tim from his fright. Christie followed him up the steps. Another scream. It came from the nursery.

"Wait here," he said, as they reached the door.

She had no plans of following him in.

Tim gazed around, and stopped when he saw a gravestone in front of the tree, on the wall. How did it get there, and more importantly, who was under it? He fished his cell phone from his pocket and snapped a picture.

Officer Bird looked hard at the image before following Tim to the nursery. The gravestone disappeared from in front of the tree.

"Now do you believe me?" Tim bellowed out.

"I never said I didn't," Bird said, while slowly shaking his head.

The crib began to shake as a rumbling sound came from behind the wall. Tim and Officer Bird tried to keep the crib still. Tim felt like he had been punched in the gut, and he fell to the floor. Pieces of the wall, where the tree was painted, fell. When it was over, it looked as if the tree had fallen onto the crib.

Bird shone his flashlight inside the fallen wall, gasped, and told the couple to go downstairs. Grabbing his wife's hand, Tim led Christie down the steps. A few minutes later, more cops were banging on the door. Tim let them in, and they joined Bird upstairs.

About a half-hour later, Bird came into the kitchen and told them a body was found inside the wall. They couldn't tell how long it has been there, but the body was of a little girl and almost fully decomposed.

* * *

Three months later Officer Bird went to Tim and Christie's new house saying they had identified the body from inside the wall. Abby Dunlap, killed by her mother, Donna, who was undergoing psychiatric treatment at Lakeshore Hospital.

Bird picked up the pacifier off of the floor, wiped it off and put it in Darla's mouth before leaving.

A Letter Of Disappointment
By Amy Karian

Dear manager of The Homicidal Homily Hotel,
I will have you know that I am deeply disappointed with your clearly false advertising. You had said in your brochures that this was a place to get away from vampires and ghouls and other paranormal creatures. You had promised me a fearfully rollicking good time. Ax-wielding maniacs and dangerous traps and secret trap doors... THAT was the good time I had in mind when I paid for my reservation.

What did I get instead? Well, let me tell you.

First night of my stay at your "esteemed" establishment —your brochure's choice of words. Not mine — I went out for a late night swim. I had assumed that the pool would be empty. But no. There was a MERMAN in the pool. Can you believe such audacity? A MERMAN!

Oh, of course, he was quite beautiful with his silver streamer hair and his siren-like singing. And he smelled surprisingly like Irish Spring body wash. Not at all like fish or seaweed.

And, yes. Of course, I fell in love with him. He was terribly charming and kind and so in need of someone to love and his eyes were like moonlight on a still lake. We had many long conversations by the pool.

And yes. Of course, I found a way to be with him and I have moved out to the ocean to live happily ever after with him.

I am writing this to let you know that I am deeply disappointed in your false advertising and blatant lies. If you wish to speak to me regarding my complaint, please write your message on a piece of paper, roll it up nice and tight, stuff it into a bottle, seal the bottle, and fling said bottle into the ocean. I will eventually receive your message and contact you.

Sincerely,
Mrs. Adelaide X

WEATHERED SPIRITS
By David Haunter

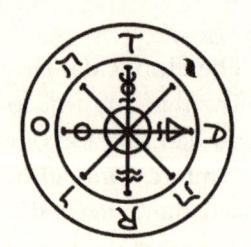

Prospect Cemetery — here and there people wandered the grounds looking for loved ones, placing flowers on graves, or simply taking in the day as the gentle breezes whispered quietly through the elms. One guy in particular seemed out of sorts, wandering from headstone to headstone, reading names and looking confused. He didn't notice the guy coming up behind him.

"You look lost, friend. Where you from?"

"Section Y. *You?*"

"Section A. No wonder you're lost — section Y's way back there. It's a big place, you know. 22,000 people buried here."

"What, you counted 'em all?"

"I sort of keep inventory."

"Sounds like a real hoot." He produced a pack of smokes from his sleeve, knocked a couple out and lit one with an ancient Zippo, offered the other to his new friend. "Name's Bobby, Bobby Fenton."

"Josh," he said, waving away the cigarette, "Nice to meet you."

"Likewise. *Hey* — any chance you could help me get back to my section? I mean, this is nice and all, but it's kinda square and long-haired around here, you get me?" he said, pointing to a middle-aged couple walking around.

"Sure. Follow me," said Josh, not really getting the reference. "It's not far."

Bobby Fenton took a long drag of his Marlboro and puffed out three near-perfect smoke rings toward the patch of blue sky overhead. He had an easy stride, a stride that said he hadn't a care in the world. A tiny pocket comb appeared in his hand and he raked it effortlessly along the greased sides of his ducktail. "What I wouldn't give for some Brylcreem. Don't suppose you got any?"

"No, sorry," said Josh. "Nice jacket, by the way."

"This? Yeah. Real leather, too," he said, flicking a finger against the sleeve, "bought it at Stedman's on Delaware Street. Ever been there?"

Josh had not.

"Tried to get a job there when I left juvie but old man Stedman ranked me out, said he didn't want no JD workin' in his store. My old man was pissed — said he'd take my Chevy away if I didn't get a haircut and a job. Some kinda bullshit, huh?"

"JD?"

"You know, juvenile delinquent."

"Ah. Sounds rough."

"It wasn't no rose garden I can tell ya that."

Ten minutes later they were back in section Y, one of the older areas of Prospect Gardens. The trees here were taller and age-worn, and the grave stones were worse for wear, overgrown and shabby. Bobby seemed relieved. "That's me over there," he said, ambling over to a rather plain square-ish marker.

Bobby James Fenton
1939 — 1957
In Loving Memory

"My folks, jeez — you think they'd have put something nicer, you know?"

"Could be worse, you could have no resting place at all, like Silent Sarah."

"*Who?*"

Josh pointed across the way to a glen of trees at the far end of section Y. Bobby looked for a few moments before he spotted her peeking out from behind a stone. "Never seen her around here before."

"She's been following us since section D. She doesn't belong anywhere — at least I don't think she does."

"Why they call her Silent Sarah?"

"She doesn't talk. The story goes that she became pregnant out of wedlock and her father tried to send her away, but Sarah refused, told her father she was going to live her own life and make her own decisions. He cut her tongue out a few nights later and not long after, she killed herself."

Bobby lit another cigarette, slapping his Zippo shut with a flourish. "That's a crazy story, man. Who told you that load of horseshit?"

Josh pointed again, this time to a nearby grave where a tall man with wild grey hair was circling around an old cross-shaped marker, fussing with it, mumbling to himself.

"Old Cross Lee? You gotta be kidding. The man's bat-shit crazy."

"No crazier than anyone else."

"Speak for yourself, man, I got all *my* marbles. *That* guy is definitely out of his tree. *Sincerely.*"

They watched as Old Cross Lee fussed with his grave, picking old leaves off it, dusting things real or imagined off the top of his marker, and doing a few more circuits around the entire plot, occasionally grabbing his hair and moaning. Some extra-sensory perception alerted him to the fact he was being watched.

"Ah, shit, he spotted us. Let's make like a tree and get atta here, huh?" said Bobby.

Josh missed Bobby's reference once more, so he ignored it. "He's harmless."

"Says you, pal."

Old Cross Lee covered the distance pretty quickly, surprising the two. He was tall, but he walked with a slight hunch, and his duster coat was right out of the civil war era. His hair was full-on wild-grey and blowing back in the breeze of its own inertia. He had his shaky hands to his lips shushing harshly. "Don't you two know better than to talk so loudly? He'll hear us! He mustn't hear us!"

"Crazy old man," said Bobby, taking his Zippo out again to light yet another Marlboro. Chain-smoking was moot when you were corporeal. "What the hell you talking about?"

"I'm talking *precisely* about hell, young man. This isn't just a resting place for the dead — it's a place to harvest their souls as well."

"Ah, you're outta your mind."

Old Cross Lee waved his arms dramatically. "The cowardly, the unbelieving, the vile, the murderers, the sexually immoral, those who practice magic arts, the idolaters and all liars – they will be consigned to the fiery lake of burning sulfur! This is the second death!"

"Dead is dead, amirite, kid?"

Josh shrugged. "I suppose."

Behind them, Silent Sarah crept closer, only a few plots away actually, listening intently to all of this. Josh spotted her, but the other two were too preoccupied with their theological discourse to notice. Bobby leaned on his stone and pointed his cigarette at the old man. "You can't die twice, you crazy old bastard. Don't you know that?"

He shook his head. "The *dead* as you call them, the earthbound spirits, the *weathered* spirits, we're only here temporarily! The great light will come, the great *crossing over*..."

Bobby made a face, pointed a chin at Josh. "You know anything about this here 'crossing over' jazz, kid?"

Josh shrugged. "Well, I've heard that spirits, earthbound ones that is, hang around because they have unfinished business."

Bobby took a long drag of his cigarette, tossed it off toward some nearby shrubs, took another one out and lit it. "Kid, I finished all my business a long time ago. Been watching this psycho mumbling over his headstone for almost 60 years..."

"64," said Josh.

"Okay 64 — so if there was gonna be a crossing over or whatever, it woulda happened already. Face it, we're stuck here wandering around and that's that, you get me? And anyway, who's to say crossing over ain't a better deal? The grass being greener and all that happy horse shit."

Old Cross Lee pointed a crooked finger at Bobby and fixed him with a cold stare. "Better the devil you know than the devil you don't know."

Just then a tiny rumble of distant thunder sounded and Old Cross Lee's eyes darted up to the swatches of blue sky between the trees. "What was that? Thunder!"

Bobby flicked his cigarette away. "I didn't hear nothing. Besides, there ain't a cloud in the sky."

The faint whiff of sulfur suddenly filled the air, and a very tall woman appeared, dressed in a business suit and holding a clipboard. She pulled her stylish glasses down to look down her nose at the threesome standing there and tsk tsk-ed. "Hm. A sorry lot this year."

"Oh yeah? Who asked ya?" said Bobby, taking his Zippo out again and lighting his umpteenth smoke.

"Name's Ashley. I apologize for the parlor tricks, but I couldn't resist. The sulfur was a nice touch, wasn't it?"

Old Cross Lee jabbed a finger at her. "I know you — you're…"

She held a hand up. "Ah, no. I'm only his executive assistant. The boss is far too busy these days to be dabbling in these mundane matters. His interests are too far-flung, after all. Arthur Johnson Lee, is it?" she said, looking at her clipboard.

"You don't fool me! Beelzebub! Lucifer! Hssss!"

"Charming, isn't he?"

"Yeah, he's a real hoot," said Bobby, casually dragging on his cigarette and blowing intricate tendrils of smoke though pursed lips.

Ashley eyed him curiously. "Those thing's'll be the death of you."

"Run it up the flagpole and see who salutes, sister," he said.

"You have gumption. I like that in a spirit. You'd be a real star back home."

"Yeah, where's that, Peoria?"

She gave a rather mirthless chuckle and then turned her attention to Josh who was standing quietly off to the side. "You, what's your deal? I haven't seen you around here before."

"No deal. Just hanging around."

Ashley pushed her glasses back up the bridge of her nose. "Right. Just hanging around."

"Hey lady, what's this all about anyway?" said Bobby. He was leaned back against his stone, casually toking on his latest cigarette, arms crossed. "You interrupted our little powwow over here. You're a pretty screwy broad if you ask *me*."

"Quite the anachronism, isn't he?"

Josh shrugged. "He can't really help it now, can he?"

"No, I suppose not," she said. "So, now that our little meet-and-greet is over with, suppose I tell you why I'm here since we haven't got a lot of time."

"Lady, you must be crazy — we got nothing *but* time."

Old Cross Lee was down on his knees straightening up Bobby's plot. "Time… time is the fire in which we burn…"

"I want your souls," she said. "I just need a couple to fill my quota for this quarter, is all. I promise you it'll be a good deal."

Bobby sucked back the rest of his smoke and tossed it into the wind, which promptly sucked it up and away in a crazy spiral. "I ain't no divinity student or nothin', but ain't hell a bad thing?"

"Hell tends to get a bad rap these days. I assure you things are quite different now. For the price of your soul I can offer you anything you like. Such as that... thing you used to drive."

Bobby got excited. "My Chev? No kidding!"

"Mm hmm. And that girl of yours..."

"Cindy! Man, I haven't seen here in a dog's age. You can do that?"

Josh stepped forward. "Don't do it, Bobby."

"Stay out of this," she said, locking her dead grey eyes on him. Something about that look made the little hairs on the back of his neck tingle.

A faint light appeared not far away, unnoticed by all concerned except Ashley who caught a glimpse of it through her peripherals. Or maybe she just felt the hair stand up on the nape of her neck. "Bobby, I promise you all you desire. Just sign on the dotted line..."

She flipped the clipboard over toward Bobby, who stared at it blankly. He saw his name on the top and writing so tiny and dense it reminded him of those musty old encyclopedias back at the Lincoln High library. "I don't know about this..."

"You have no choice, Bobby. If you're waiting to cross over to that *other* place, you'll be waiting a long time. Remember that bottle of Boone's Farm, that joy ride down route 22 at 3 AM, remember killing your girlfriend that same night...?"

"Hey. I... didn't kill her..."

"Not directly, no. But who drank that whole bottle of whiskey? Who got in the car and drove it down that lonely highway when they were seeing double? Who lost control of that same car and rammed it into a utility pole?"

Bobby took the clipboard.

"Bobby, you have a choice. Don't listen to her," said Josh.

The light grew brighter. This time it caught the attention of Bobby and Josh and Old Cross Lee. Ashley produced a shiny red pen and handed it to Bobby. "Forget it. You'll never get in. You're a sinner, Bobby. Come with me — you won't regret it. But you must hurry. *Sign it.*"

Old Cross Lee got up, started to walk over to the light and the others watched him go, even Silent Sarah, who was crouched down behind a granite stone as he went by. "The light is no place for a child of the darkness," he said to her as he faded away.

Bobby dropped the clipboard. He backed away toward the light. "I remember now. It was after the pep rally at Lincoln. I drank a whole bottle of hooch, it started raining, I crashed the car, and…"

"And you killed that girl, yes." Ashley stepped forward, her features swirling and swimming in a strange kind of kaleidoscope. "Bobby, my patience is wearing thin…"

"Cindy ain't *dead*. I remember now…"

"Bobby…"

It came back to him like a forgotten dream; the blurred lines on the road, Cindy's Coty perfume filling the interior of the car, the rain-slicked windscreen, the skidding, the squealing tires…

…throwing his body across Cindy just before… before…

While she was distracted with Bobby, Silent Sarah appeared and clamped her teeth into Ashley's arm, uttering guttural snarls like a wild dog.

Bobby ran for the light.

"Get off me, you cur," said Ashley, batting Sarah away. "Look what you did! You ruined a perfectly good suit."

Sarah got back to her feet, opened her unholy maw and screamed an unearthly silent scream, her truncated tongue quivering and undulating. Josh tried to look away, but found he couldn't.

"Aren't you charming," said Ashley, brushing her ruined sleeve, which suddenly knitted itself back together somehow. "Go away, you horrid thing."

She batted Sarah away with the flick of a hand, momentarily changing form. Where one moment there was the tall woman in a business suit, the next there was a grotesque abomination without form surrounded by dark flames, and then back again. Josh thought he imagined it, it was so quick.

The blink of an eye. Maybe half a blink. Maybe no blink at all.

Ashley was still brushing her suit down as she walked back to Josh, primping, pushing her glasses back up her nose, making sure her hair was still in a tight little bun atop her head. "Well that was interesting, wasn't' it?"

"Where'd everybody go?" asked Josh.

"Your two friends? They went 'upstairs', to my chagrin. And I haven't reached my quota. I'm not happy about that."

Josh shrugged.

She reached down and picked up her clipboard. "Anyway, there's plenty more where they came from. After all, the two surest things in life are death and taxes, am I right? There's a sucker born every minute, and one dying, too. The cosmic ballet goes on, does it not?"

Josh shrugged again.

"Your communication skills are dreadful. Ugh. See you in about 73 years, Mr. Josh, give or take a year. Maybe *you'll* sign on the dotted line *then*, hmm?"

"Don't bet on it."

She blinked out.

* * *

"Josh. *Josh!* Hey!"

It took him a few moments to refocus, some guy shaking his shoulder, calling his name. It was Harry.

"You okay, kid? What are you doing over here? We're supposed to be over in A section. We got tons of landscaping to do and you're over here messing around."

Josh shook his head. "Sorry, Harry. I was just looking at some of the headstones here."

Harry scratched his ear, made a face. "Yeah, well we got work to finish. Come on. You can daydream on your own time."

Harry marched off, leaving Josh standing there looking down at the square-ish stone with the name Bobby James Fenton etched into it.

It was nice meeting you Bobby. Hope all is well. Say hi to Cindy for me, if she's there.

He hustled up to Harry who was walking at a brisk pace and already out of section Y.

From way back in the oldest part of Prospect Gardens, crouched behind a mossy and faded headstone, Silent Sarah watched them go.

BETTER THAN BEETHOVEN
By Michael Haberfelner

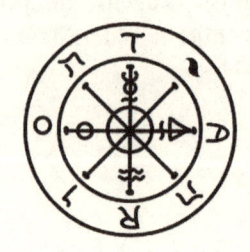

"What would you have done in my situation?" he asked his bust of Beethoven musingly. Yes, Hubert had a bust of Beethoven standing atop his piano, just like that blond kid, Schroeder, in that *Peanuts* comic strip. It was a gift from his mum, to encourage him to never give up playing. It was supposed to be authentic, too, back from Ludwig Van's times (or thereabouts) – but be that as it may, it looked quite a bit too gaudy for Hubert's taste. But hey, at least she didn't give him Liberace's candelabra.

"What indeed would you have done, maestro?"

"First of all, I wouldn't have played them such a tacky melody."

Hubert almost fell off the piano stool hearing this. Of course he had talked to the Beethoven bust – but he had never ever expected a reply. After all, he wasn't crazy, and busts don't talk. He wanted to say something, but nothing came out and instead he just stared at the thing, eyes wide open.

"Oh come on, have you never seen a talking bust before?"

Still, not a peep out of Hubert.

"Ok, stupid question, of course you haven't."

"Who... who are you?"

"You mean to tell me you've got my bust on your piano and you don't know who I am?"

"You're Beet-... no, it can't be?"

"And why not? For all intents and purposes the real me's dead as far as I know. So why would you deny my immortal soul the right to possess my own bust?"

"But... but..."

"You can but me all you want, young man, but that won't answer your question."

"Question?"

"You wanted to know why you failed at that audition, remember?"

"Oh... that."

One can forgive a certain forgetfulness when someone has just found out that one's Beethoven bust is a sentient being, and not only that, it is in fact Beethoven – even if Hubert didn't have the faintest idea if any of this was real. He wanted to believe though, as the alternative would be he was hearing voices inside his head, and that wasn't something he would have been very fond of. So he listened.

"Your melody, it was tacky."

"No, it was not!" Hubert always took immediate offense in this sort of criticism, not in the least because there was a grain of truth in it. "It was an only seemingly simple tune that obscured the intrinsic melodic complexity of the piece as a whole and..."

"Oh, damned be all music theory. We had none of that shit in my time, you know."

"I'm not yet finished!"

"And you are already doing with your monologue what your piece did with your melody, build up a lot of smoke to hide its tackiness."

"It's called compl-..."

"I don't care what it's called, a rose is a rose."

"And what would you know?"

"What, apart of being one of the most renowned musical geniuses of all time? A man who wrote some of his best work when he was totally deaf? Need any more qualifications?"

"I don't even know if I believe you're Beethoven."

The bust sighed. "So what did the panel say?"

"In a nutshell, they liked the melody, but..."

"Not good at reading between the lines, are we? 'Like, but' means they hated it."

"I prefer to see it as constructive criticism."

"And I call it failing at your audition."

"Ah yeah, and what would you do?"

"Well, at first I'd chuck out that stupid melody, and then..."

* * *

This night, Hubert twisted and turned in his bed as if he was a washing machine on spin cycle. Was the bust on his piano really Beethoven? Of course not, because that would be stupid. And yet… there was another audition at the institute next month, and he could really do with that grant. And he could also really do with some help, that piece he played for the panel the last time – oh, he loved it when he wrote it, but the more he thought about it, and the more he talked with Beethoven… no, with the bust, the more he talked with *the bust* about it, the more he came to the realization that all he really had was just a tacky melody buried beneath a ton of intellectualized bullshit. Why hadn't he realized that sooner. So let's just assume for a moment, this time around he actually had Beethoven to help him to compose something new – what on earth could go wrong? Nobody could blame him for learning from the best, and that others weren't given his chance wasn't really his fault. Besides, nobody would believe he was secretly talking to the long-dead Beethoven anyway. Sure, he had no guarantee he wasn't just hearing voices, but even if, if it got him through the audition, fine, and if not, he could label himself insane after the whole thing. It was worth a shot for sure.

And with that thought, Hubert finally fell asleep, smiling.

* * *

"How did you like that, maestro?"

"It's beautiful – and perfectly dull. Scrap it!"

"But how can it be dull, can't you hear what I've done here?"

"I can hear it, and I don't like it."

"But… but…"

"Who's Beethoven, you or me?"

* * *

"How about that one?"

"If I wasn't already, I'd swear you want to bore me to death."

* * *

"What do you think about this one?"

"I think I wish I was alive again – just to be deaf again."

* * *

"What a piece of crap that was!"

"But I've spent hours on it…"

"Hours you won't get back, my boy. Ever thought about an alternative career plan to making music?"

* * *

He had tears in his eyes when he started to play his latest composition. He thought everything would be easier with Beethoven (he was by now sure the voice from the bust was the real deal) by his side, but with the audition less than three weeks away, he hadn't written a single piece, heck not even a single note the maestro had liked. What's worse, under Beethoven's harsh treatment, Hubert's self confidence had gone out the window. Still, after he had finished his new piece, he looked at the bust full of hope, as if this was the piece to break his curse. The bust remained silent.

"And?" Hubert tried to egg on the bust.

"Crap."

"But how can it be crap? Can't you see that I've done the exact same thing that you've done in the Missa Solemnis?"

"And that's why I call it crap."

"But the Missa Solemnis…"

"Why, can't you see what you're doing? In all your compositions you just try to emulate my style, and by doing so you completely forget to find your own voice."

"But I thought…"

"I know what you thought, you thought being me would solve all your problems and make you the next Beethoven. But I'll tell you a secret, if I had spent all my time copying Mozart and Haydn back in the day, I wouldn't have lasted five minutes. And nobody would have heard of me now. And heck, I'm pretty sure nobody would have manufactured this bust of me – and without that, where could my soul have gone?"

"So you're saying…"

"Don't be me, be you! And I'll guide you every step along the way."

* * *

The following days, Hubert felt re-invigorated, the shackles of trying to emulate Beethoven removed gave his compositions a much better flow. What he adopted from his bust buddy though was his disregard for music theory – and suddenly, when he no longer felt forced to write "an only seemingly simple tune that obscured the intrinsic melodic complexity of the piece," he found the freedom to write what he felt within himself, and it felt wonderful. Even better, Beethoven liked what he did. That was good of course, but not perfect. You see, he liked it – but he didn't love it. Sure, he didn't say even one mean thing about Hubert's composition anymore, he even dropped little compliments here and there, but to say he was enthusiastic would be a blatant lie. So day-in and day-out, Hubert tried to perfect his composition more and more, but none of his efforts seemed to please the maestro enough to say more than a few words that sounded more like nicely meant than actually nice.

* * *

One week to the audition: Hubert had made steady progress, but at the same time had the feeling he was going nowhere. And with that, his old frustrations and his self-doubt returned. And then, when he played his melody for the umpteenth time, the Beethoven bust suddenly interrupted him.

"Why don't you play a B flat there?"

"I beg your pardon?"

"Well, you know what a B flat is?"

"Of course I do, but you can't play a B flat there."

"Why not? Would it break your finger to hit that key?"

"Well, no but…"

"Then you can play it."

"But it goes against all rules of harmonics…"

"Blah blah blah. Now pray tell, in how many biographies of great composers have you read 'he was really good at the rules of harmonics'?"

"In none, but…" That was true, but partly because Hubert was never big on reading biographies of any kind.

"Well, then stop contradicting me already and try it!"

Hubert played his melody again, and put a B flat where the bust had told him – and it sounded like crap.

"I told you it wouldn't work."

"Play it a few more times. I guarantee it will grow on you."

Hubert did as asked, and if the B flat dropped into his melody grew on him, he didn't notice. His disappointment didn't go unnoticed by Beethoven.

"Well, you're doing it all wrong. You can't leave the B flat to its own devices, throw in a few C sharps and E flats to help it out a little."

"But… harmonics."

"Good God, kid, have fun a little. Throw all rules of harmonics out of the window and start to live!"

* * *

With only a handful of days to go, Hubert's composition was taking shape. It was different from anything else, but at least for

Hubert, who lived and breathed the piece, it was the best thing he had ever written. Sure, harmonics didn't play into the thing anymore, and it was full of random cadences and rhythm changes, but in Hubert's mind, it made perfect sense nevertheless. And what was better, Beethoven was enthusiastic about it, and Beethoven couldn't be wrong, now could he? Hubert knew he had a winner on his hands, the grant was as good as his.

* * *

Having played his piece, he turned to the panel expectantly. Their mouths stood collectively agape, but as much was to be expected, this music was new, it was bold and unprecedented. It took a moment for the members of the panel to collect themselves, then one of them said, more to himself than to anybody else "what the fuck was that?" – and this is where it dawned upon Hubert that something was wrong. The panel members gave each other confused looks, whispered to one another, then finally their chairman turned to Hubert.

"Excuse me, Mr. Schmittlechner, was this supposed to be a joke?"

This caught Hubert totally by surprise, so much so that he found himself unable to answer.

"You know, we really liked the piece you played last time, it had a certain Beethoven vibe to it. It wasn't quite grant-worthy yet, but would you have worked on it... But the piece today..."

"Was this even music?" one of the other panelists interjected.

* * *

Back at home, a beaten and battered Hubert played his piece once more – and with all the enthusiasm, excitement and adrenaline gone, he managed to for the first time actually and objectively listen to it – and it was total crap, just random musical notes mixed together into a sour soup.

"Why... why did you talk me into this?"

But the bust didn't answer.

"Why didn't you hear this is crap? Why didn't you warn me?"

But the bust remained silent. In fact, it would never talk again.

And Hubert? Well, he never sat down at a piano again, he gave up all his dreams to become a musician let alone composer. In fact, he lost all interest in music as such. Eventually, he wound up living a perfectly miserable long life as a bookkeeper, and his contributions to the human race were forgotten only weeks after his death.

"And the bust?" I hear you ask. Oh, it was never actually possessed by Beethoven, because that would have been preposterous. But neither was Hubert just hearing things. In fact, it was possessed by one of Beethoven's contemporaries, a wine merchant called Waldefried Ammerhäuser, who had a knack for playing elaborate pranks on people, something for which he was loved by some, feared by others, despised by many, and it was this pastime that eventually cost him his head when one of his ruses accidently killed one of the lesser members of the Austrian Imperial family.

How his soul got into the Beethoven bust I don't know, it might have been Black Magic or a deal with the Devil, or really just his last, most elaborate prank.

It should also be noted here that said Waldefried Ammerhäuser had, throughout his life, not a musical bone in his body.

BLOOD WITCH
By Mike Cooley

I reached to my right and picked up the glass pint jar. Dallas was pointing his 357 at my head from across the room.

"You gonna throw that at me? I'll shoot you in the face."

"Big man. Little gun." I smiled. A soft, blue phosphorescence enveloped the fingers of my hand, beneath the jar. "How did you get in here, anyway?"

Anger crossed his face. "I'm not fucking around, Melody. You know what you did."

The jar in my right hand started to fill with warm liquid. "What I did? You mean stick up for my friends against racist assholes? Warn them of the future? Turn you down?"

"What are you doing?" Dallas' hand trembled. His eyes were drawn to the jar.

I looked at the crimson fluid filling the jar from the bottom up. "I told you I had powers. But you didn't believe me." The air in the room grew still and crackled with energy. There was a faint smell of hyacinth.

"Powers? What's in the jar? How are you doing that?" Dallas' face grew pale and his hand was visibly shaking. He was having trouble keeping his gun level. His brown eyes showed fear like a car accident in a mirror.

"It's blood, Dallas. Your blood. You better get your bitch-ass out of here before I take all of it."

"That's impossible!" He staggered toward me, his hand unclenching. The gun dropped to the carpet, but it didn't go off.

The jar in my hand was full and threatening to spill over. I set it down on the smoked-glass table and took a step to my left.

Dallas staggered by, dropped to his knees, then looked up at me. "You fucking bitch." He was shivering and his face was pale.

"You will never touch me. You are trash. Come near me again and I'll take the rest of it." I smiled, keeping an eye on the revolver in case he made a move for it.

"Blood?" His eyes widened.

I nodded.

Dallas got to his feet and continued past me, giving me a final, hateful look as he opened the back door of my apartment. "This ain't over, bitch!"

"Oh, it's over. You tell your inbred friends all about it." I picked up the jar of blood and handed it to him. "This is yours. Good luck getting it back in."

* * *

After Dallas left, staggering away, holding his jar of warm blood, I got ready. I changed into a nice pair of cutoff blue jeans, a gray shirt with a white pentangle on it, and then tucked the revolver into the small of my back, with the barrel snugged in beneath my belt. I grabbed my well-worn custom tarot deck, slipped it into my front right pocket, then brushed my raven hair back behind my ears. My green eyes flashed with resolve, as I painted my lips purple. Time for a drink.

I had been in Santore for almost a year by that time, and I knew it was nearly time to cross another small town off my list. There were only so many eerily accurate palm and card readings a girl could give before paranoia and suspicion crept into the townsfolk like fog. And the women were growing jealous of the way their husbands looked at me. I could never stay anywhere very long. I had lost track of all the faces and places.

I gave the room one last look, admiring the art I had collected, and remembering all the nights I had spent telling people things they wished they hadn't asked to know. I slipped a black leather jacket on, and then left my small apartment on foot, locking the door behind me. I knew, if things went south, that I didn't need to come back. I traveled light. I knelt down and tied my boots on tight, in case I had to run.

It was dusk, and the summer air was warm. Main street was as busy as it got, which was not very. I walked the four blocks to the

Capital Bar—The Cap, as the locals called it—and pushed the wooden door open.

It was crowded, for a Tuesday. I scanned the faces, as they scanned my body. It was mostly men, and they were mostly leering, as men do. Some of them recognized me from around town, and some of them showed the curiosity of not remembering me. I recognized a few of the women from readings I had done. The bartender, Nate, gave me a quick nod then slid a bottle of absinthe down the old, worn, wooden bar toward an empty stool near the back corner. Then he slid a glass down, which came to a stop, neatly in front of the bottle.

"Thanks, Nate." I walked across the room, feeling the eyes following me, most of them locked onto my breasts or ass. The magnum was obscured by my leather jacket, which was adorned with silver studs on the back in the shape of an upside down cross. A few of the men whistled and made crude remarks to each other about things they would never get to do to me. One of the women made a furtive sign of the cross behind my back.

I sat down in front of the absinthe, the liquid inside was the color of my eyes. I poured myself half a glass and sipped on it. The taste lingered on my tongue, bringing back eighty years of memories that popped to the surface like bubbles in a dark sea. The bar smelled like old beer, ashes, and dashed hope.

Charlie was up on a shelf behind the bar, curled up in a ball. He opened one eye and looked at me. His hair was black and spiky, in constant disarray.

I tapped the bar and blew him a kiss. "Hey, Charlie. It's good to see you again."

He stretched big, then smoothed his black fur and jumped off the shelf onto the bar. Then he sauntered over, like a leopard in the jungle, and climbed onto my shoulder, nuzzling against my neck and purring. He was the size of a kitten, but never got any bigger. And his eyes stayed blue, like a newborn. I could feel his heartbeat in my mind, like a butterfly flapping its wings.

Nate came over, looking around the room habitually, checking for signs of trouble. "How are you, Melody? Everything good?"

I smiled. "No worries, Nate. You hear something?"

Nate smiled, revealing yellowed, chipped teeth. "The usual rumors going round. You know the story." His hair was greased back, and it looked like he hadn't shaved for a week. It was obvious from his face, which side he slept on.

"That I'm a witch, bent on stealing all the womenfolk's husbands?" I laughed. "No thank you."

I slid Nate a Benjamin. "This is for your trouble."

"You're no trouble, Melody. You always brighten my day. And you're too pretty to be a witch." Nate winked and then slipped the bill into a pocket.

"Most days, I'd agree with you."

Someone at the far end of the bar started waving their empty beer mug comically, like he would succumb to thirst if it wasn't refilled immediately. Three guys at another table started yelling for refills in drunken, boisterous voices. Nate shrugged, looked in that direction, and then wandered that way.

* * *

I sipped the green liquor, savoring the burn, and let feelings from all around wash over me. I drew an octagon on the wood of the bar with my forefinger, tracing over and over the lines until it lit up with a dim ocher fire. The alcohol helped shroud me from the unclean thoughts of the rabble, and the sharp edges of jealousy and lust.

I was halfway through the bottle and feeling fine when I heard the click.

"Blood Witch!"

I turned to my left on the stool. Dallas was standing twenty feet away, his face a ghostly pale. He raised a shotgun and pointed it at me.

I darted left and reached behind my back for the revolver. The blast was deafening and I could feel pellets rip through my jacket and shirt. I was bleeding. But most of the shot missed.

Time slowed.

I raised my left hand, aimed, and pulled the trigger. The 357 lurched in my hand, and there was a loud bang. I could smell gunpowder and fate. My ears were ringing.

Dallas' face lit up in surprise. The bullet hit him right above his left eye. His hands unclenched and the shotgun hit the floor shortly before he did.

Most of the drinkers hit the floor. Glasses shattered as they dropped. Nate ducked down behind the bar. One guy at the far end of the bar raised his glass and took another swig. Several of the women screamed in harmony.

I pulled another hundred out of my pocket and slipped it under the bottle of absinthe. Charlie was still sitting on my right shoulder, seemingly unaware that anything was wrong. His claws held onto my jacket tight.

"Sorry, Nate." I got up and walked out, pausing to look down at Dallas, cooling in his own blood. I shook my head, wiped off his revolver, and then dropped it on the floor next to him.

"Everything's bigger in Texas…even the idiots."

Charlie looked down, shook his head, then blinked his blue eyes.

I stiff-armed the door and stepped out. Inside, the deathly quiet after the echo of gunfire faded erupted into commotion. I pulled open my jacket and surveyed the damage. My shirt was ripped and a handful of pellets from the shotgun blast had gone clean through my skin. The blood was quickly fading, like the pain.

I pulled the map out of my back pocket and crossed off Santore. The map was full of towns that had been crossed off over the years. The moon was rising. I walked south, toward the edge of town. I could feel the eyes upon me, from doorways and windows. I could feel their fear and their relief as they watched me go.

I held up a hand, and gave the whole town the finger as I walked. I could still hear the wanton thoughts of men watching my ass, like rats in the walls.

Charlie began to purr.

For Love of the Trees
By Harpalyce Wilde

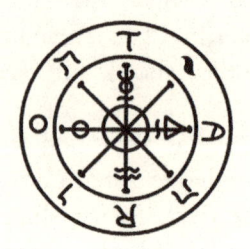

"Come back, Delphina! Please! Let me explain!" Karya's final words echoed in my memory as I stepped from the boat to the island.

It had been three decades since I'd fled from her, from the grove upon the hilltop. But regret burned in me as fresh as ever. Today, I hoped to change that.

* * *

I'd met Karya just after completing my master's degree, while traveling solo through Europe. Athens was a city built upon history — you couldn't dig a single square foot of it without hitting ruins or artifacts. It was full of folklore too — which it was my business to collect before it faded from aging memories. My favorites were stories of love between mortals and supernatural beings. Love was a mystery to me — I'd long sought after its meaning but never truly experienced it.

Karya had approached me one evening as I was dining alone in a smoky tourist taverna in the shadow of the Acropolis. She'd wanted to practice her English — she told me she was applying for a position as a tour guide and it needed to be perfect. I'd agreed, and in exchange I asked her to tell me all the old tales she could recall.

And so, she had. She'd gifted me with tantalizing and obscure folklore such as I'd always yearned to discover, and I eagerly transcribed it. Ancient myths, painted with fresh and vivid detail. Of Narcissus, the self-absorbed boy who'd been transformed into a flower, and Daphne, the beautiful girl who had shunned Apollo. Of Odysseus' many trials on his journey home to his Penelope. Of the lust of Zeus, and how many lives he'd ruined. Of the wrongs that had turned

Medusa so dark and destructive. Each story was brilliantly told; as if she'd experienced it firsthand. When the live music began at midnight, she pulled me to my feet and we danced together.

That night, we'd chased the music through every club in the Plaka. And then we watched the sun rise while sipping bitter Greek coffee in a sleepy café. She told me of her work as a future-preservationist — collecting seeds of plants and trees, against the time when they would no longer grow in their native lands. How the world was changing around us, and how we had to be ready to change along with it.

Days turned to weeks as we explored the faded wonders of the ancient countryside together, collecting seeds and stories. By then, I'd fallen completely for her, and she seemed just as enchanted by me. I followed her home to her small island, expecting to meet her extended family in the single village that clung to its rocky shore. Braced for awkward conversations from unwelcoming relatives about our unconventional arrangement.

But instead, she'd taken me up the steep hillside, following an old goat-track. As we climbed, she spoke of the local spirit who kept watch over the island still, though her name was forgotten by the folk who dwelled there.

At the summit, we came to a little glade of gnarled, ancient trees where the ground was spongy with layer upon layer of hazelnut shells that gave off a rich, earthy aroma. Inside the grove, the silence felt so deep, it was as if the world hadn't changed in thousands of years. She showed me the ruins of the hilltop temple, a pile of tumbled, mossy stones that had once been surrounded by a sacred hazel grove.

It was there in the cool shade that she finally told me what she really was. Led me to "her tree", as she called it. It was the most ancient and gnarled, ancestor to all the others. It might have been three thousand years old.

I thought she meant it was her favorite. But when she touched the trunk and suddenly vanished from sight, I figured it out. It wasn't "her tree". It was... her.

She stepped out a moment later, beaming at me with her charm turned on full. "So? What do you think?"

I'm ashamed now that I was spooked. Horrified. Stunned. I ran from her, heedless to her pleas. I stumbled down the steep hillside to the little town, and paid a boat to take me straight back to Athens. Got on a plane and flew home to my aging parents, back to the safety of my boring home town. Put her stories and my sketches of her — all the mementos of our brief time together — into a bonfire after months of drowning in wretched depression. Hoping, praying to forget.

I couldn't face it — what I'd seen. I wasn't prepared to be in love with a hamadryad. It felt as if I was living through one of those stories I'd chased. But somewhere deep inside, I always wished I'd been braver.

* * *

Today, as I retraced our long-ago journey up the winding goat-trail, I encountered an ugly, modern villa where the hazel grove had grown. Besides the house and its half-acre of sculpted, irrigated landscaping, the hilltop contained nothing but arid stones and scrubby brush. Not even a stump remained. Thirty years of change — I was too late…

I dropped to my knees, my pent-up tears pattering in the dust like raindrops. My fingers dug into the hot, barren dirt, seeking the earthy loam I remembered. "Oh, Karya… I'm sorry!"

The ground began to tremble beneath me, and a cool mist sprang up. When I blinked my tears away, the modern villa was gone and rising in its place was the temple — not the ruins I remembered, but a sparkling white marble building with graceful columns. A grove of vigorous hazel trees surrounded the temple and the sweet scent of flowers perfumed the evening air.

Slender and youthful, just as I remembered her, Karya stepped from within a tree trunk and came to me. Took my hands in hers. "Delphina? Is that really you? You came back…"

She pulled me into a fierce hug, and I wrapped my arms around her, clinging tightly. We drank strength from each other, as if a single embrace could erase our decades apart. But when our joy at being reunited was spent, she pulled away and turned her back to me.

"What is it, my love?" I felt tears prickling my eyes again, threatening to fall. "I'm so sorry I ran away. I was a fool, then. But I swear, I got smarter. We can be together now, if you still want that. If… if you can ever forgive me."

Karya turned to me and smiled, but her leaf-green eyes were mournful. She touched my cheek, wiping away the moisture. "My dearest, I forgave you long ago. It wasn't your fault, it was mine. I rushed ahead, and you weren't ready." She sighed and bowed her head. "But, this has to be goodbye."

"Please! I don't care about what you are. It doesn't matter! I only care about *who* you are and the friendship we once shared." I knew I sounded desperate, but I couldn't help it — I was an aging folklorist with a wreckage of a life, twice divorced, with no kids and no close friends. "In the time we've been apart, I've been haunted by the music of your laughter, by echoes of our conversations, and… and… the curve of your cheek as you smile. Every time I close my eyes, there you are, in my dreams. You are my one, my only love — I know that now. And I'm so sorry it took me this long to realize it."

"Delphina, they chopped down my grove. My tree is gone." Karya gripped my hands, anguished. "It means that I can never return to the mortal realm. And you belong there. You must go back now, before it's too late."

Grief and incredulity shook me. After all my doubts. After all my courage, coming back here and baring my soul. She was rejecting me, sending me away. I couldn't let her do that. After a lifetime of hunting for love, and half a lifetime of feeling empty without her, I refused to let her do that, no matter how noble her intent. If she didn't want my affection, I might as well swim out to sea until I could swim no more. "Please. Don't send me away. It doesn't matter where we are, so long as we're together."

"Oh… Delphina, my beloved." Her sigh was husky with sorrow and acceptance. The whisper of breeze through the hazel branches grew louder, and the heavy air reeked of honey and salt sea and flowers. "If that is what you truly wish, then come with me." She led me to the crown of the hill, to a sheltered spot overlooking the village far below. As the sky painted itself mauve and violet, Karya wrapped her arms around me, pulling me close.

I clung to her and she to me as we watched Venus rise with the new crescent moon, heralding the dawn. Together, we swayed gently to the rhythm of unheard music, the eternal tides of nature rising to surround us with their soothing ebb and flow.

* * *

When sunrise turned the sea to beaten copper, a goat herder on the island discovered two stately hazel trees growing with branches intertwined. Growing atop the ancient hill where, the day before, no trees had been.

And to this day, the village storytellers swear most solemnly that if you visit the young grove of hazels when the moon is new and Venus rises to greet the sun, you might catch a glimpse of them. The lovers, dancing together in their timeless embrace.

Out, Damn Spot!
By Mandy White

The spot has grown larger. At least I think it has. Maybe my eyes are playing tricks on me. Maybe it's my mind playing tricks on my eyes. I just don't know anymore.

It's been nearly three weeks since I first noticed the spot. I was lying in bed before lights out, glaring at the ceiling as I have done every night since I arrived here.

My first thought was that the brownish-yellow spot looked like a water stain from a leaky roof but of course that's impossible in this place. Day after day, night after night the strange blotch on the ceiling has mesmerized me, commanding my attention day and night, even after the lights are out. I sense its presence even in pitch darkness; it emits some sort of invisible energy, like a thick phosphorescent glow that I sense to the very core of my being instead of merely seeing it with my eyes.

What the hell is it?

After the first week it began to grow, the edges rippling and undulating like a puddle of water lapping at the cold gray ceiling. It seemed to feed on my anger; I noticed that the fouler my mood, the faster the spot grew.

I was able to reach it by standing on my bed. The spot was warm to the touch and my fingertips detected a slight buzzing sensation. Was it a burn mark? Perhaps it was an electrical wire shorting out in the ceiling. Faulty wiring wasn't uncommon in old buildings such as this one.

Sometime toward the end of the second week the spot had enlarged to the edge of the room and begun to spread down the wall. I began to get the feeling it was coming for me, to swallow me into wherever it came from.

I tried telling the guards about it but they just laughed and told me to shut up. They didn't see any spot. They denied my request to be moved to a different cell, calling me crazy before resuming their never-ending poker game. I had no neighbors to confide in. The whole block was… well, dead. Except for me – the sole occupant of death row at that particular time.

The more I stared at the ever-expanding blemish on the ceiling and wall of my cell, the angrier I became. I was angry at my situation, at the people responsible for putting me there but most of all I was angry at the spot itself. How dare it invade my private space? What did it want?

One morning after I finished my breakfast I lost my temper and threw my coffee cup at it. I expected the plastic mug to rebound and rattle to the floor but instead it just disappeared. I swear it did, as God is my witness. It vanished without a sound as if swallowed by quicksand.

I caught a lot of shit for that one. The guards didn't believe my explanation even though they tossed my cell twice and didn't find the missing mug. They are still convinced I have it hidden somewhere.

Standing on my bunk, I reached up to touch the spot where the cup disappeared. To my surprise, the ceiling was no longer solid. My fingers slid right through the concrete as though it were soft butter. My whole hand disappeared past the wrist. I groped around but found nothing but an empty void on the other side.

Today, the spot is large enough to accommodate my entire body and I now know what I must do. I am going to follow that cup to wherever it went. I have no future here. I've just been served my last meal. Tomorrow is execution day, or E-Day, as I have come to know it.

I'm leaving, but not on a jet plane. Don't know where I'm going but I won't be back again. I ain't sticking around to be put to death for a crime I didn't commit. Ok, I admit I DID kill a man but it was justified. He had it coming for fucking my wife. I served justice in an unjust world and this is the thanks I get for it.

The spot ripples like water in a breeze, calling to me. It's my way out of here, I'm sure of it. I don't know if I will find the regular world on the other side but if I do you can bet I'll finish what I started. After all, it takes two to tango. That S.O.B. couldn't have slept with my wife if she wasn't willing. She won't get away with it if I can help it.

"I'm coming for you, Rosalee! You hear me? I'm coming for you!"

* * *

She sat with her head down and a wadded tissue clutched in a shaking hand. She dabbed at her eyes from time to time; not out of grief for the man who had just died from lethal injection but for the other who had died at his hands. Her ex-husband was an evil man and she was glad he was dead. Rosalee had attended the execution to see for herself that without a doubt he was gone forever. Maybe now the nightmares would stop.

Kevin hadn't handled the divorce well. When she remarried, he lost his mind.

She would never forget the day she returned home from a shopping trip to see a barrier of yellow police tape surrounding her home and the ominous sight of a coroner's van parked at the curb. When they wheeled out a gurney carrying a black plastic body bag she collapsed, wailing in anguish.

Rosalee knew Kevin was the one responsible for Troy's death and he gave the police no resistance when they arrested him. In court, he said nothing in his own defense despite his court-appointed lawyer's insistence that an insanity plea would be in his best interest. Kevin's silence was almost as good as a confession.

Now, the monster that had made her life a living hell and destroyed her second chance at happiness was dead. Rosalee knew she should be feeling relief as she stood on shaking knees but she was still rattled from witnessing the last moments of her ex-husband's life. The nightmares were still fresh in her mind – the much-too-real vision of a hand emerging from the ceiling of her bedroom, reaching, groping as if searching for her. And then there was the plastic cup that had inexplicably appeared on her bedroom floor one morning. Who had put it there?

As she waited for the guard to escort her back to the prison's front entrance, Kevin's voice still echoed in her head. Those last words he shouted just before losing consciousness from the injection:

"I'm coming for you, Rosalee! You hear me? I'm coming for you!"

CRAWL SPACE
By Juliette Kings
aka The Vampire Maman

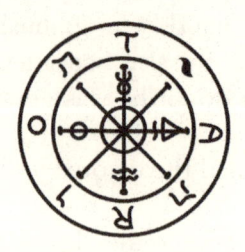

I took off my sweater and handed it to my brother Aaron. There was no way I was going to crawl on my stomach under the crawl space of a house with it on.

"So, tell me again why you can't get the bodies out from under the building first?" I had to ask.

"They're not quite dead yet and they might attack Austin. He's human, a Regular Human," my brother told me. Austin, by the way, is a Regular Human and sometimes Vampire Hunter and usually just a guy who does a great job restoring old buildings that seem to be filled with scary shit like ghosts and old musty Vampires.

And of course, Aaron was wearing a $5,000 suit; of course he couldn't crawl under the house.

"You might know them," added Austin, meaning the creatures under the house.

I almost gave him a fang-filled snarl, but I just gave him a weak, normal girl smile.

Wearing garden gloves, I crawled on my hands and knees over bare dirt. Even in the dark, I could see assorted bugs and cobwebs. Rat droppings were scattered around. Why the crap would any Vampire want to sleep under floorboards?

About 20 feet in, I was at the boxes. OK, whatever, they were coffins.

I thought back of when I was a kid, and always the one to crawl under houses and into tight spaces. It wasn't because I was small. It was because I pretend to be fearless, and now it is because I don't take any bullshit from Shadow Creepers and dusty old Vampires who can't deal with the modern normal world. We're not having a Nosferatu and Dracula Hoedown, kids, this is the 21st Century.

The lids were on the boxes. I managed to kneel without banging my head on anything and pushed one off. Inside was a male in a pinstripe suit. His face looked pale and waxy. I noticed sunken cheeks and lips that seemed a little thin. He hadn't fed in a while. The box next to him contained a female. Skin stretched over her face, a hint of teeth including fangs showed beneath parted lips. Oh come on, all Vampire girls know not to sleep with their fangs exposed. She wore some sort of black dress thing. The scent of rotted roses and cigar smoke came from her box. In the third box…nothing jumped out. It was another male. I recognized the face. His eyes, open a bit and yellow-green, rolled to stare at me. I saw recognition in his face; a face that was once handsome and could be again, but he was so strange, so weirdly in the shadows and cold, not like Vampires I associate with, but like a dead fish.

Then my butt vibrated. My phone. I pulled it out. Garrett, my darling 18-year-old son, calling from college. I'm a mom. I must answer.

"Hey Mom, what do you call two ducks and a cow?"

"What?"

"Quackers and Milk."

"Good one. What do you call an Englishman, two ducks and a cow?"

"Graham Quackers and Milk. Love you, Mom."

I heard a groan from one of the boxes. I slap-slap-slapped it hard with my hand and hissed at it. The noise stopped.

I kept my eyes on the yellow-green orbs that continued watch me as I talked to my son. He rattled on about classes and girls he knew and sang me a song he wrote. He said he went to the beach almost every day and was going to go surfing on Sunday. He said it was the perfect college for Vampires. He was so excited about school. My heart melted a little.

Then he asked me what I was up to.

"I'm under a building with three boxes full Shadow Creeping Vampires. You know me, every day is Halloween."

"How'd you end up there?"

"Helping your Uncle Aaron and a friend. Long story, but the short version is that I was the only one wearing jeans and I'm smaller than they are so I got elected."

Old Green Eyes started to sit up. "I gotta go, Garrett. I'll call you back later today."

"Love you, Mom."

"Love you too, sweetie pie."

I looked at my old friend. OK, he wasn't a friend. I'd met him before, a long, long time ago.

"What are you doing here?" I said, trying to keep myself from sneering at him. "You look like a fucking Zombie. What is wrong with you people? Have you lost all self respect?"

"Juliette," he whispered my name in a dry voice, like old coffee grinds and gravel.

"Jasper. That last time I saw you was… 1923, New Orleans. What are you doing here?"

He started to tell me something in French that I couldn't quite make out when I stopped him. "Listen, you have three choices. The first is that you agree to live like Modern Vampires and stop this nonsense of lurking around like you've just come out of some creep show. The second is that I leave you to the Vampire Hunters. The third is that you let one of my friends, and I use that term loosely, take you to San Francisco where you can be with others of your kind. But you can't stay here. We have enough problems in Sacramento without your kind."

"My kind?" He opened his eyes wide and showed his fangs.

"That is exactly what I mean, you giving me the evil eye and trying to scare me with your ugly mug. You used to be handsome and well, you were never charming, but you used to be, well, not THIS."

I crawled back into the sunlight, which was no cup of tea, believe me. I might spend time during the day outside, but the sunshine, especially after the darkness under a house, always comes as a shock. I pulled out my sunglasses, put them on, then took a deep breath and brushed off my pants. Filling Aaron and Austin in on the situation, I told them that I'd let them decide what to do with Jasper and his friends.

I needed to go home and take a shower and scrub my skin off with steel wool, or at least that was how I was feeling. The image of his eyes stuck in my brain like Poe's *Tell Tale Heart* story.

"*It is impossible to say how first the idea entered my brain; but once conceived, it haunted me day and night. Object there was none. Passion there was none. I loved the old man. He had never wronged me. He had never given me insult. For his gold I had no desire. I think it was his eye! Yes, it was this! He had the eye of a vulture — a pale blue eye, with a film over it. Whenever it fell upon me, my blood ran cold; and so by degrees — very gradually — I made up my mind to take the life of the old man, and thus rid myself of the eye forever.*"
— *Edgar Allan Poe, The Tell-Tale Heart and Other Writings*

His eyes will haunt me for sure. Maybe I'll check on him in a few months' time, out of morbid curiosity. That is, if the Vampire Hunters or other creatures don't get them first. There are Shadow Creepers who seem so vile, but then there are other Vampires who I don't even dare name or ever seek out for any reason.

Like I said, Halloween is never far from my reality.

I called Garrett back. He listened to my story. I didn't make it into some cautionary tale or anything like that. We just talked. He told me that I was the most awesome mom ever.

NEW EMOTIONS
By R James Turley

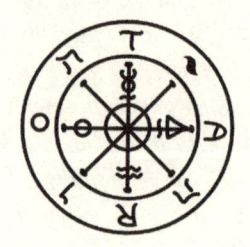

Stars blanketed the night sky. Mid-Autumn was Dani's favorite time of year. The crispness of the air. She loved looking up on a clear night, trying to count the stars. There were always too many to count.

It was just after 9:00 PM. Dani was gazing at the stars and having a cup of coffee when she saw the most unusual set of lights in the sky. She knew they weren't stars. Half oval in shape, the lights seemed to be drifting down to the Earth.

Dani finished her coffee, grabbed a flashlight and started walking in the woods behind her house toward the lights. The farther into the woods she walked, the lower the lights appeared. Whatever it was seemed to stop and hover just above the tree line. In an instant the lights vanished.

Dani shone the light to the sky. Nothing but twinkling stars. She was starting to question if she really saw what she saw. She had heard stories of UFO sightings that turned out to be someone's imagination. You heard a lot of that, living in the country.

Dani turned to head the mile or so back to her house, but stopped when she heard branches break. The ground shook beneath her. A small earthquake? Even though they weren't common in Pennsylvania, it had happened before.

Dani thought she saw a human silhouette run past in front of the light. Who would be in the woods at night? She stared at the heavens. Could it really be? Dani had always believed in UFO's and life on other planets. It was so arrogant to think Earth was the only planet in the universe with life.

Dani hid behind a tree when the sound of crunching leaves got closer. As she peeked out of her hiding spot, her hand hit the tree, knocking the flashlight to the ground. When she bent to pick it up, she saw a hand reaching for it.

"Here you go," an unseen voice said.

Falling back in a start, Dani said, "Who said that?"

"I did," and a man's face came into view from the light.

Dani stood and snatched the flashlight from his hand. He was tall, about six feet, and wore a flannel button down shirt and blue jeans.

"Where'd you come from?" she asked.

He looked up, and pointed to the brightest star in the sky.

"I'm Dani," tapping on her chest.

"My name is Yen." He gazed through the darkness, "It's nice to be back here."

"You've been here before?"

"Yes. Many times," Yen said, looking into her eyes and nodding.

Dani took his hand, "Come with me."

As they walked, Dani tried not to, but couldn't help staring at him. Not because he was someone from outer space, but he was the most gorgeous guy she had ever seen. His dirty blond hair stretching just past his shoulders, and the twinkling of his light brown eyes. Dani instantly fell in love with his eyes. Not how she expected aliens to look.

Yen was happy to be back on Earth, the first time in twenty-five years. He had studied a lot of humans on his countless journeys to Earth, but never one as beautiful as Dani. Her long, wavy brown hair shone under the moonlit night. Yen felt something he had never felt before.

He sat on the couch, drinking the tea Dani had offered him while they talked. He debated on telling her everything, since she already knew he came from space. On his previous visits, Yen had landed in secret, just like he'd planned this time. Yen hadn't expected anyone to be in the woods.

The longer they talked, the closer Yen felt to Dani. Yen excused himself, and walked out the back door. He sat on the top step, and gazed up at the stars. The door opened and Dani sat next to him.

"What's the matter?" she put her hand on his.

Yen shook his head. "Ever since I saw you, I've been drawn to you. I don't know how to describe it." He pulled his hand out from under hers, "And when you put your hand on mine, I get chills."

Dani smiled. "I like you too."

"Is that what it means?" He stood and walked down the steps. "I'm not supposed to have these feelings."

"You don't have feeling on your planet?"

"Not really," he said, looking down.

Dani stood up. "Your parents didn't love each other?"

Yen put his hands in his pockets, "We don't have that emotion, or we're not supposed too. Maybe I've been coming here too much."

She frowned, "So sad."

Yen finished his second cup of tea, and went to his space pod for the night. Space travel always made him a little queasy. He laid there in the dark thinking about what Dani said. She made it sound like he, and the rest of the planet's children missed out on something. He started to think that he did. A world with love sounds inviting.

Yen didn't leave the ship for two days, nor did he sleep very much. The prospect of asking Dani to go back to Trendar with him scared, yet also excited him. Those emotions were new, too. Somehow, giving in to those emotions felt right.

The next morning, Yen returned to the house. Before he could knock on the door, Dani opened it. Even barely awake and with her hair messed up, she was still the most beautiful creature he had ever seen. Yen knew for sure he wanted to explore the emotion of love with her.

"Hi." Dani smiled, showing off a dazzling smile. "I missed you. Come in. You want some coffee?"

"What's coffee?"

"It's like tea, but stronger and better."

She chuckled at the face he made after sipping the hot beverage. "Here, give me," Dani poured it in the sink. "I'll make you some tea." she filled the teapot.

"Thank you," Yen smiled at the thought of making a face. "Tea would be better."

Dani sat across from him, and asked about Yen's home planet. He was willing to answer any question she asked. After a few minutes of being bombarded, to which he never got the chance to answer, Yen held up his hand to stop her.

"Would you like to come with me back to Trendar?"

* * *

After waking up from hyper sleep, Yen contacted his best friend, Ambrose, who worked at Skylab, the landing spot. It was at the foot of the Hippo Mountains, not far from Yen's home city of Qusi.

He went over and assisted Dani, not sure how she would react to waking up after two years. They sat in the cockpit and prepared for landing.

"Hello, old friend." Yen shook Ambrose's hand. "This is Dani." he motioned toward her. "The girl I told you about."

"Nice to meet you," Ambrose nodded. He turned his gaze to Yen, "You're going to have a hard time convincing the Queen of your new found emotion. We aren't supposed to have real emotions."

"I have to try," Yen scratched his head. "It feels like these feelings are going to bubble over from my soul."

"Love makes everything worth it," Dani added.

Yen opened the pod for Dani to get in for the short journey to Qusi. A night at Yen's quarters before reporting to the Queen, in Lance – something he wasn't looking forward to. An anxious feeling came over him, another new emotion. It was almost overwhelming.

He smiled when he caught Dani gazing around at the scenery. From the mountains in the background to the tall green trees in front, she looked like she loved what she saw.

"It's beautiful here." Dani pointed at the trees up ahead.

"It is, here, in this part," he motioned to the trees. "The other two parts are not. One is a dessert, and the other is all frozen."

Yen continued to explain to her, as he pulled the pod next to his quarters, about the planet. Trendar was divided into three parts: Twilight, night and day. Only twilight was habitable. The planet had no rotation, so it stayed twilight all the time. Nothing lived in the day and night because of the extreme temperatures.

Yen let Dani go inside ahead of him. She pointed up at the wall in front of her. "I love your row of hourglasses."

"Thank you." Yen turned to look at her, "It's how we measure time." He pointed to the row, "There are twenty-six, and when they fill up, they flip over to start a new time cycle, or day, as you call it."

The Queen didn't look happy when she saw Dani walking with Yen. He was still trying to figure out how to explain why Dani had come back with him, and his newfound feelings.

"Step forward!" Queen Lucinda bellowed. "Who is she, and why did you bring her back with you?"

Yen gulped, "This is Dani," and motioned to her. "I'm having feelings I've never experienced before."

The Queen made a face and asked, "What kind of feelings?"

"Love, your highness."

"Impossible!" she yelled. "We don't have those emotions."

"Maybe we should." Yen was brave. "Dani has been telling me how nice it was to have parents who love not only each other, but their children."

The Queen stood, not looking happy. "Arrest them!" She pointed.

Yen grabbed Dani's hand and raced out of the castle before the guards could catch them. Jumping in the pod, Yen headed for the other side of the Hippo Mountains, to the city of Torro. Ambrose had a house just inside the city line.

After picking up some supplies in Torro, they were going to hide out at the Glass Sea on the border of the restricted Day Area. It was constantly daylight there, and too hot for anything to live.

When they arrived at Ambrose's, four of the Queens soldiers were waiting to take them into custody. How could Ambrose betray his friend that way?

Three days sitting in a small room in the dungeon, Dani was regretting her decision to come to Trendar. Yen did his best to cheer her up, but nothing worked. She longed for home.

They stood as the Queen walked through the door. She looked inquisitive, stopping before Dani.

"Be seated," the Queen said. "Tell me more about growing up with love from your parents." She sat beside Dani.

Dani regaled her with childhood stories of how her parents supported, and loved her unconditionally. One of her favorites was when they surprised Dani with a trip to Disney World for her eleventh birthday. She had the time of her life. Dani had a birthday party with Snow White and the seven Dwarfs, her favorite book. Also, the way they had supported Dani when she refused to dissect a frog in high school.

The Queen reached toward Dani and grabbed her hand. "Is this what love feels like?"

Dani nodded. "And so much more."

"Hello," King Bradford walked through the door. The three of them stood.

The King motioned for them to sit, and sat beside Yen.

The King turned to the Queen, "Did you say anything yet, Lucinda?"

She shook her head, "I was about to when you came in."

* * *

Two days later there was a double ceremony in the courtyard. All the guests celebrated the new Love Liaison, Dani. The wedding ceremony was festive, and happier than any other wedding.

Books by WPaD:

Deviant Shadows: Tales of the ParAbnormal
Weirder Tales: An Omnibus of Odd Ditties
Strange Adventures in a Deviant Universe: WPaD Science Fiction
Creepies: Twisted Tales From Beneath the Bed
Creepies 2: Things That go Bump in the Closet
Creepies 3: Nightmares on Deviant Street
Goin' Extinct: Tales From the Edge of Oblivion
Goin' Extinct Too: Apocalypse A Go-Go
Dragons and Dreams: A Fantasy Anthology
Passion's Prisms: Tales of Love and Romance
Tinsel Tales 2: Holiday Hootenanny
Tinsel Tales: A Holiday Treasury
Nocturnal Desires: Erotic Tales for the Sensual Soul

WPaD books are available worldwide in paperback and ebook.
For more information, please visit our website:
http://wpad.weebly.com/
Find **WPaD Publications** on Facebook
for updates on our upcoming projects
Or follow **@wpadpublication** on Twitter.

Meet the Authors

Diana Garcia
Marla Todd
Mandy White
Juliette Kings
Michael Haberfelner
Mike Cooley
Harpalyce Wilde
Lea Anne Guettler
J Harrison Kemp
David Hunter
Allison Ketchell
Debra Lamb
Amy Karian
Soleil Daniels
R James Turley
Dave Henderson
Brian Callahan

Deviant Shadows
Tales of the ParAbnormal

By WPaD
(Writers, Poets and Deviants)

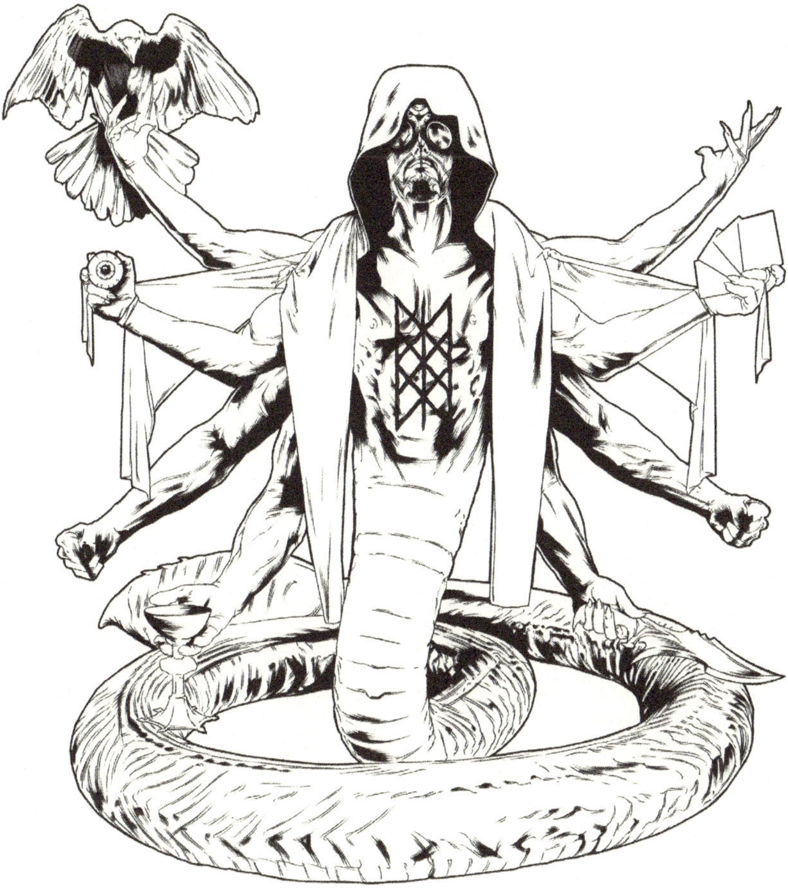

Made in the USA
Las Vegas, NV
08 September 2021